HEADING UPTOWN

MARISSA PIESMAN

HEADING
Uptown

A
NINA FISCHMAN
MYSTERY

**Delacorte
Press**

Published by
Delacorte Press
Bantam Doubleday Dell Publishing Group, Inc.
666 Fifth Avenue
New York, New York 10103

ISBN 0-385-30537-0

Interior design by Christine Swirnoff

Manufactured in the United States of America

AUTHOR'S NOTE

Many people helped me with ideas and information for this book. These include Lori Brennen, Elaine Budd, Suzanne Cogan, Shawn Coyne, Ellen Count, Brian DeFiore, Mary DiStephan, Jackie Farber, Eleanor Hyde, Ronnie Greenstein Kravitz, Lita Lepie, Diane Ouding, Jane Rosenberg, and Bernice Selden. I am indebted to them all. I am also grateful to my agent, Janet Wilkens Manus, for her guidance and unending enthusiasm, and to my husband, Jeffrey Marks, for his loving support.

HEADING UPTOWN

. . . .

Funerals brought out the best in her mother, Nina thought, as Ida narrated their way through Queens. Nina and Ida Fischman were on the 8:32 to Great Neck, en route to Helen Hirsch's funeral. Ida was going on and on. She had a tendency not only to meander but also to verge on the nostalgic. Which was hopeless when it came to activities requiring crisp optimism, like picking stocks, but just perfect for all death-related activities.

Nina's mother was great at visiting terminally ill patients, comforting bereaved relatives, and warming you up for the funeral of someone you hadn't seen in quite some time. Ida was a natural historian who knew how to throw in enough fiction to keep up the dramatic tension. And she was replete with details, like a big fat colorful nineteenth-century novel, inching forward slowly. Not like those anemic postmodern books people turned out these days, written in black and white. Ida's narrative line, like her waistline, was ample.

And like those Victorian novelists that got paid by the

word, Ida's stories let you tune in and out without missing any important plot developments. Right now Nina had taken the opportunity to fix her attention on Shea Stadium, outside the grimy train window, since Ida seemed to have gone off on a tangential subplot involving the deceased's sister-in-law.

"I hope you're taking this all in," Ida snapped. Like any good narrator, she could tell when she was losing her audience. "Don't forget that you're the executor of Helen's will."

The streets of Flushing blurred as Ida's words came sharply into focus. "Holy shit," Nina said.

"You forgot, didn't you?"

"Well, it was a long time ago." Nina remembered now. Helen Hirsch was a college friend of her mother. Helen and Ida had been Hunter girls, back in the thirties, when the smart sons of immigrant families went to City College and the smart daughters mostly went to work. Except for the persistent ones who somehow managed to talk their bewildered parents into letting them go to Hunter. Which meant a year of mandatory Latin and a chance for you to meet young women from German Jewish families who lived on West End or Park Avenue. These women would invite you to their homes occasionally and you would be in awe of the crystal and china and the impeccable English of their parents, who had subscriptions to the opera and the Philharmonic. And then you would go back to the Bronx and be filled with impatience at the Yiddish accents and the Yahrzeit glasses that served as the Baccarat of the boroughs.

Helen and Ida had lived through this together and this mutual coming-of-age had served to forge a bond that had remained unbroken. When her mother got together with her friend, Nina was always amazed at the changes that came over the two of them. They seemed to bestow upon each other the rosy romantic expectations of prewar New York City. Varicose veins would deswell, osteoporosis would recede, spines would straighten, chins would lift, and Helen and Ida would girlishly chat about the moving primitivism of Diego Rivera and the agitprop drama of Clifford Odets and whatever else was hot in the autumn of 1939. If women friends could have a song, like married couples in old movies, Ida and Helen's song would be "You Make Me Feel So Young."

They never seemed to discuss the mundane—money problems, physical ailments, marital or parental crises. Yet they must have, in private, since Ida could always give a quick summary of what was really going on in Helen's life, between the folk dance classes and the gallery lectures. Over the years Nina hadn't really paid close attention to Helen Hirsch's history. She never paid that much mind to Ida's middle chapters, waiting for her mother to get to a plot point before truly listening. And here they were at a major plot point. Nina was the executor of Helen's estate. This had happened because Helen had died childless.

Dying childless seemed to Nina to be an issue of her generation, not of her mother's. Nina knew she wasn't the only one who skipped to the bottom of the obits, looking for the reassurance of someone who had seemed to live a rewarding existence without leaving any offspring. The childlessness seemed like uncharted territory. There were few role models for this sort of thing. All of Ida's peers, no matter how dried up and bloodless, seemed to have managed to couple and reproduce at least once. Nina scrutinized their faces, searching for a vestige of the radiance that pregnancy and young motherhood might have once brought. Hard to believe, especially since so many of her own peers seemed to remain childless no matter how juicy they were.

Helen Hirsch had not always been childless. She too had coupled and reproduced. Only once. And her son had died.

Mark Hirsch was still alive when Helen had redrafted

her will. She had sold the two-family house in Flushing soon after her husband died, and had moved into a rental apartment on Queens Boulevard. In helping to rearrange her assets, the family lawyer had suggested she write a new will. Mark was named as executor, but Helen needed an alternate, in case her son was unavailable at the time of her death.

Nina recalled the conversation, especially the way Helen had said "unavailable." Instead of having morose, predeceasing overtones, the word seemed to raise all sorts of romantic possibilities. Because that was the kind of guy Mark Hirsch was. If he was unavailable, it wouldn't be because some disease had struck him down prematurely. It might be because he had changed his identity or because he just didn't feel like being available. He had been quite the juvenile delinquent, driving too fast, cursing too much, and dropping too much money at basement poker games. To Nina, who was almost ten years younger than Mark, he had been overwhelmingly sexy. After a visit to Flushing, eight-year-old Nina would daydream about him for weeks.

Helen had asked Nina's permission to name her as the alternate executor. Nina had said yes. She always said yes to her mother's friends. Actually they made very few demands on her. Nina thought this might be because Ida ran interference for her. She had a suspicion that her mother was always telling her friends, "Oh, Nina's not that kind of lawyer," or "She wouldn't know anything about that; it's the age of specialization, you know." But wills and estates were things that Nina knew about.

Nina worked for an organization called Legal Services for the Elderly, which meant drafting wills for the endless stream of old ladies who sat patiently on folding chairs in the waiting room. She didn't mind the drafting, since it was a one-shot deal. You got the thing witnessed and the client was out of there. Now, being an executor was something else.

"What does that mean?"

"Direct testimony. That means you have to give very brief answers, because any topic you raise in your direct testimony can be subject to cross-examination. Get it?"

"Try me."

"Okay. Now, Mark was Helen's only child, right?"

"Right."

"What was Mark's wife's name?"

"Beverly."

"Beverly Hirsch?"

"Of course. Remember, they're older than you. They got married over twenty years ago. Women all changed their names back then. Besides, she's not really the type to keep her name. You'll see what I mean when you meet her. I mean, meet her again. You've met her before. I'm pretty sure you went to the wedding, didn't you? But you probably haven't seen her since. Correct me if I'm wrong."

"Ma, you're not playing by the rules. Monosyllabic answers, please."

"Sorry, I'll try harder."

"Okay. Now, Mark and Beverly had kids, right?"

"Just one."

"And what's the kid's name?"

"Lisa."

"How old?"

"Fifteen, something like that."

"And when did Mark die?"

"Well, I'm not sure exactly when he died. You see, the whole thing was so odd. He had been missing for a while; I can't remember how long. Helen was already on chemotherapy when he disappeared. That I'm sure of. Because she was tearing herself up and I was very worried about her. She started treatment right after her birthday, which was in October. And we're in February now. So I guess . . ." The conductor appeared to announce that the train was pulling into Great Neck station.

"This is hopeless, Ma. You're just going to have to fill me in after the funeral. And remind me never to put you on the stand."

2 . . . .

The Great Neck train station had a sort of Tudor charm.
When you first arrived, you could almost pretend that you
were in a small English village, that Miss Marple might walk
by with a wicker marketing basket. But as soon as you hit the
parking lot and saw the Mercedes gridlock, you knew you
were a stranger in a strange land.

The funeral parlor was right across the street from the
station. Ida and Nina entered and were directed to the
Hirsch service. Her mother pointed out Beverly, causing
Nina to clutch Ida's arm.

"Is this normal?" Nina whispered to Ida.

"You mean black leather at a funeral?" Ida asked. "I
guess in some circles."

"Yeah, you mean like the people who hang around the
S&M bars down on West Street? Maybe there's some Nassau
County branch of the Mine Shaft that Beverly Hirsch fre-
quents." Nina had never gotten used to leather clothing.
When leather pants became the rage on Columbus Avenue,

they seemed unnatural to her. Instead of looking fashionable, they made people look like adults who had never been toilet trained.

Maybe it was just sour grapes, because leather pants were not something Nina could even consider. With her figure, she had to draw attention upward. Other women achieved this by a gaily colored scarf or dramatic earrings. Nina achieved this by never shutting up.

It took a while for them to work their way over to Beverly. As soon as they had walked into the room, Ida was surrounded by a throng of oldish ladies who all looked vaguely familiar to Nina. She had trouble telling them apart, since they each had gray hair and carried a Channel Thirteen tote bag. Ida introduced them one by one, each time explaining their connection to Helen Hirsch.

Some were cousins, some were former teaching colleagues. Others were women who had just hung out with Helen, going to museums and plays and sometimes abroad. They weren't rich, they weren't well-dressed, but they were attractive in their own gray-haired, flat-shoed way. They seemed to know about Nina, that she lived on the Upper West Side and was a lawyer. They asked reasonable questions about her job and her travels. And when Ida explained to them that her other daughter, Laura, had been unable to attend because she couldn't find anyone to take care of the kids at the last minute, they shrugged, as if taking care of kids was just one of life's activities and not a holy crusade. It was a rare feeling to be in a crowd of aging Jewish mothers and not feel self-conscious about being single.

Nina managed to keep Beverly in view, which was easy because Beverly had a good eight inches on the old ladies. When she got close, she realized that at least four of those inches were attributable to Beverly's high heels. She had an undeniably great body. Her legs were long and her leather skirt was short enough to reveal a well-developed calf and thigh musculature. Beverly Hirsch could have been a diagram in *Gray's Anatomy*.

The long black leather jacket hid the rest of her, but Nina would put money on a flat stomach and great delts. There was something about the face, though, that was less than spectacular. Nina wasn't sure what it was. The hair was good, insofar as it was big. Big black hair, tumbling down around her padded black leather shoulders. And a big red mouth, outlined in an even deeper red. And big diamond stud earrings, to go with the big diamond tennis bracelet and the big diamond ring and the big gold Rolex watch and the big red nails. Or maybe the diamonds were actually cubic zirconia and the watch was purchased from some Senegalese guy on the street and the nails had been pasted on. Nina couldn't tell. But whether everything was real or not, it was all big.

Except the nose. Beverly had made the mistake of having a nose job too early, before the plastic surgeons had grasped the concept of subtlety. So swimming in this sea of bigness was a too-small nose. It wasn't the nose, thought Nina, that lost her the most points. Nina was, after all, a New Yorker, and had gotten used to those odd little cartilage vestiges set at such awkward angles on the faces of the city's ethnic women.

It was Beverly's eyeglasses that were unforgivable. After all, a nose job was something you were locked in to. You had gone to some guy on Park Avenue back in the early sixties, when he was practically the only game in town. And he had done, with the limited technology available to him at the time, the best he knew how. And now you had to walk around with this porcine look and there was nothing you could do about it.

But glasses were something you could just take off. And they had become a hot fashion accessory, now that the baby boom demographic bulge was losing its eagle eyes. Armani himself had jumped on the bandwagon. These days there were frames that could make you look intelligent or interesting or even beautiful.

Beverly's frames were big (of course) and had a little DIOR pasted onto the lens. Nina remembered this as a particularly idiotic fashion fad from a few years back. Nina expected something more au courant of Beverly. Maybe something oversize and Italian. Probably contact lenses.

That was it, of course. People who were really vain wore contact lenses so extensively that they couldn't even bear to be fitted for new frames. So on the rare occasion when they couldn't put in their lenses, they had to go rummaging around their drawers, looking for eyeglasses that were by now hopelessly out of date. That must be the case here. Hard-core vain.

It was time to stop looking at her and start talking to her. Ida guided Nina over to Beverly and introduced them. The accent, like everything else, was big. Unclear, however, which borough it had come out of.

"Sure, I remember you," she said to Nina. "You were at our wedding. You must have been around Lisa's age. You lost a lot of weight."

It often struck Nina that women who seemed capable of only limited mental tasks in most situations could retain information regarding other people's weight for years, sometimes decades. Unlike genuine idiots savants, they couldn't tell you that December 13, 1972, had fallen on a Wednesday. But they could often tell you, within a pound or two, how much you'd weighed that week.

"I didn't really lose it," Nina said. "It just sort of redistributed itself. Aerobics helps."

"Tell me about it." Beverly dentalized, blunting her *T*s. You didn't get to hear that too much on the Upper West Side.

To Nina it evoked both warmly nostalgic and repellently grim memories of her own borough childhood. "Aerobics is my life."

Nina believed it. "How's Lisa?" Ida said, breaking in, apparently anxious to turn the conversation away from weight. A wise move. There was no point in discussing such topics with a Great Neck aerobics bunny. But it was the sort of losing proposition Nina often found herself signing up for.

"She's having a very hard time." Beverly lowered her voice to Ida. "First her father, and now her grandmother."

"Poor kid," Ida said.

Beverly stretched an arm over Ida's head and pulled her teenage daughter over. "Lisa, you remember Grandma Helen's friend Ida, don't you?" The child nodded. "And this is Nina. She's Laura's sister. Laura's the one that's married to the dermatologist that your cousin Brooke goes to in the city."

Nina noted that time was passing. Brooke Shields was now old enough to have Jewish adolescents named after her. "Nice to meet you," she said to Lisa.

Lisa smiled back, but she looked very unhappy. It was understandable, considering the circumstances. But her misery did not look situational. It looked deeper, more permanent. Nina wasn't surprised. For one thing, the child was not thin. She wouldn't go so far as to say that Lisa was fat. But she was definitely not thin.

And Nina knew how hard it was to be not thin even on the Upper West Side, where people had graduate degrees and liberal politics. It was hard, even with a mother like Ida who didn't dye her hair and was plump as a pigeon herself. It was even harder to be not thin on the Upper East Side, where people wore Chanel and often voted Republican. Which was probably why Nina had always kept her zip codes in the 10023–10025 range. But it must be hardest of all to be not thin in Great Neck with a mother who wore black leather to your grandma's funeral.

Lisa was chubby and miserable, but aside from that she was rather pretty. Lively eyes, thick brown hair that Beverly kept pushing away from her daughter's face, and skin that was probably the envy of her cousin Brooke.

A funeral official appeared in the doorway. Nina sensed that this might be the last opportunity she would have to talk to Beverly. "I'm sorry to have to bring this up," Nina said, "but I am, as you might know, the executor of Helen's estate. And I don't have a copy of her will. Do you?"

Beverly tapped her long red nails together. They gave off a synthetic sound and Nina decided they were probably fake after all. "I don't know," Beverly said. She turned to Lisa. "Do we?"

"I'll check on it," Lisa said.

At that moment the funeral director whisked the Hirsches into the next room. Beverly waved her nails at Nina, mouthing "see you later."

"That was odd," Nina said. "She asked her fifteen-year-old daughter if they had a copy of the will."

"Actually it makes sense," Ida said.

"What do you mean?"

"I think it's almost time for the service to begin. Do you want the condensed version of the Beverly and Lisa story?"

"Why bother? You know you're incapable," Nina said. "We'll discuss it tomorrow." Nina knew that Ida wouldn't be up to much for the rest of the day. Helen's funeral was bound to take a lot out of her. It was never easy for her mother to say good-bye to another Hunter girl. Especially one that was being replaced by an android dressed in black leather. Ida did seem pretty broken up during the eulogy. But then the Channel Thirteen tote bag brigade closed in on her again and they passed around some old photographs and anecdotes and just generally shot the shit in a sweetly supportive way.

Nina hoped she would be as blessed at Ida's age with old friends who were around to console each other. So far her track record wasn't good. Susan Gold, Nina's oldest friend, had been murdered last year by a man she'd met through a personals ad. And the last Nina had heard from her college roommate, Linda was living in Phoenix with four sons and was on antidepressants.

3 . . . .

The following evening, Nina decided to make risotto. Why she had chosen today to cook was unclear. She wasn't having company and making risotto was not something she did often. Or ever, for that matter. But she had somehow found herself in possession of a bagful of arborio rice, and for months she'd been trying to convince herself that it would be nice to put aside thirty-five minutes and just stand at the stove and stir constantly. But it always seemed like too big a sacrifice.

Nina's idea of cooking was mixing together a bunch of stuff in a pot (after maybe sautéing an onion if that was absolutely necessary), bringing it to a simmer, and going off for an hour to write checks or do her back exercises. It certainly wasn't being tied to the stove with a wooden spoon in her hand. But listening to her mother for thirty-five minutes was something of a sacrifice also. Combining the two seemed like a brilliant idea. She settled in on the kitchen step stool, with two cans of College Inn chicken broth on the counter, and called her mother.

"Okay," Nina said, when her mother picked up. "Tell me about the Hirsches."

"Hold on a second. Let me get an emery board." So her mother was as bad as she was, having to do two things at once. Nina thought back to her college years, when she had been able to do no things at once. Unless you counted staring at Jimi Hendrix posters to be doing something. That eighties decade had really ruined everybody. Thank God the age of overachievement had ended. But remnants of this compulsive behavior would crop up, she thought as she stirred and stirred. Maybe there should be a twelve-step program for this.

"Let's see, the Hirsches," her mother said, filing her nails. "When Mark was born they were living in an apartment in Queens. Rego Park, I think. Though neither Helen nor her husband grew up in Queens, of course. No one my age grew up in Queens. It was still farms before the war." Nina knew enough not to take Ida literally about the farms, that seventy-year-old Jews described a place as being farmland when they were trying to avoid using the word goyim.

"Where were they from?"

"Helen was from the Bronx and Jack was from Brooklyn. He was a union organizer, very good-looking and charismatic, with all that thick wavy hair that all the radicals had back in the thirties. They were married during the war and Mark was born the year after his father got back. Soon after that, Jack was purged from the union."

Nina knew what that meant. "Party member?"

"Oh, yes. Pretty high up. He was a great speaker; he could talk anyone into anything. In the late forties a lot of these unions started cleaning house, and Jack Hirsch was a casualty."

Nina had heard similar stories from her parents over the years, mostly about schoolteachers and loyalty oaths. "So what did he do?" she asked.

"He was unemployed while Mark was little, and Helen had to go back to teaching. I think that's why they never had another child. After that Jack opened up a hardware store somewhere in Queens. Farther out, toward Nassau. And that did okay, and they bought a two-family house in Flushing."

"That was the same store he owned when he died?"

"Yes, it was. I always got the sense that Jack felt somewhat defeated, hiding his light under a bushel selling hardware. And Helen probably regretted not having another kid, though she really did like her job."

"And Mark was a juvenile delinquent," Nina said, remembering him with slicked-back hair and tight black jeans.

"He was a sweet little kid. They didn't have any trouble with him until high school, when he got in with this crowd that gambled a lot. His parents were always breaking up poker games in the basement."

"I'll bet that's not the only thing they were breaking up in the basement."

"You're right. He went out with a lot of girls. Helen was always afraid he would knock someone up."

Nina added some chicken stock. She was getting into this risotto thing. You added small amounts of liquid over and over again for a long period of time, like gardening. And you had to wait for the payoff. This could be good training. Since she didn't have a garden, maybe she should make risotto regularly. Then she could graduate to Zen meditation, something she'd always been very bad at. "Did you ever make risotto?" she asked her mother.

"What's that?"

"That Italian rice that you have to be very patient with and stir constantly for an eternity."

"Why would I want to do that? I already raised two children."

Her mother had a point. Was risotto simply Nina's latest child substitute? "Anyway, I'm sorry I changed the subject. You've been very good, not digressing at all," Nina said. "Please continue."

"Okay. Mark was never a great student, but he was a smart enough kid and he got into Queens College. He joined one of those things that are like fraternities, but aren't quite. What do they call them?"

"House plans," Nina said. There was no point in having fraternity and sorority houses in city colleges, since everyone lived at home. House plans were a cheaper version, providing a place where commuter students could hang out during the week.

"Right. So instead of going to class, he used to hang around at this house plan place and play cards all day. You can imagine how Jack and Helen felt."

"I can imagine. Helen always fancied herself quite the intellectual."

"She did," Ida said. "All those classics courses in college. The last thing she expected to raise was a son like Mark."

"I'd say Jack was just as big a snob as Helen in his own way. Arguing all that ideology that no one else had thought about for decades."

"I guess so. Anyway, they were both disappointed in Mark's low grades and lack of academic interest. But that didn't mean that Helen wasn't wild about her son. Don't forget that he was, like his father, extremely charismatic."

Nina thought back to a Sunday afternoon in the early sixties. The Fischmans had gone to visit the Hirsches and Mark had just gotten his driver's license. He pulled up in the car in front of the house. She thought he was just the sexiest thing she'd ever seen. She had felt lust, pure and simple, even though she was only eight. She had been trying so hard to act grown-up and attract his attention, which was ridiculous, of course. And then her little sister peed in her pants and Nina had just wanted to die.

"So it had become clear to everyone," Ida continued, "including Mark, that he was wasting his time in school. He heard about a job out in Las Vegas selling air-conditioning systems and he took off."

"Well, Las Vegas must have been about as far as he could get from disappointed leftist intellectual parents in Queens," Nina said. "Besides, it had the advantage of a lot of great poker games."

"Right. Helen wasn't thrilled, but she didn't get really upset until he told her that he was going to get married before he went. That really got to her. Mark had always had girls in and out of the house and she never took them seriously. But one of them had apparently convinced him to marry her and take her with him out West."

"And it was Beverly."

"Right."

"Which was why Helen was upset."

"Need I say more?"

"No, I get it."

"According to Helen, Mark and Beverly always fought a lot. But they managed to stay married for more than twenty years. And Mark did quite well in sales out there. There was a lot of money to be made and I guess he had as easy a time talking people into buying air-conditioning systems as his father had talking workers into unionizing."

"When did they move back?" Nina shifted the phone to her right ear and the wooden spoon to her left hand. This listening-stirring combination was getting uncomfortable.

"Not until Beverly got pregnant. She had never been too enthusiastic about having a child. And when she found herself about to give birth, she wanted to move back East to be near her mother."

"What's her mother like?"

"Vain. Mean. Stupid. You know the type."

"Wears high heels even though she's already broken a hip?"

"Exactly."

"Must be genetic," Nina said.

"Your generation is obsessed with genetics. Don't environmental influences count for anything anymore?"

"Ma, you're a dinosaur. What happened after the Hirsches moved back East?"

"Mark got a job on Long Island selling heating and ventilation systems. And they had Lisa, who Helen adored. And Beverly swore she'd never have another child."

"Why not? After all, tummy tucks are no big deal these days."

"I guess she wasn't crazy about motherhood. Besides, big shot, who are you to talk?"

Her mother was right. Ida couldn't very well show her friends snapshots of a pot of risotto at its first birthday party.

"Then Jack died," Ida continued, "and Helen sold the house and moved into an apartment on Queens Boulevard. And Mark changed jobs and got involved with something to do with real estate investments."

"How did he do at that?"

"Pretty well, I think. I'm not really sure. Helen wasn't the type to brag about how much money her son was making."

"But give her a niece who had gotten into Yale and she could be insufferable."

"I guess you're right," Ida said. "Anyway, he must have been making money, because they bought a house in Manhasset Hills, on the fringes of Great Neck. Which seemed to calm their marriage down."

"I'll bet it did."

"They seemed to have some good years after that, though Helen was always worried about Lisa, who was chronically unhappy."

"Of course she would be," Nina said. "Her mother probably had her in black leather diapers."

"Probably. Anyway, everything seemed to fall apart at once. Mark started having severe business problems. Helen was diagnosed with breast cancer and had surgery. She seemed to be okay for a while, but then had a recurrence and needed another operation. She was back on chemo when Mark disappeared."

"What do you mean, disappeared?"

"It was unbelievable, really. I'd never heard of anyone just disappearing like that. Leaving your wife and child, your business partners, your mother, without any idea of where you've gone. Characteristically, it's not very . . . um . . ."

"Jewish. It's not very Jewish, is that what you're trying to say?"

"I suppose."

"Haven't you ever read any of that stuff about the abandonment rate on the Lower East Side at the turn of the century?" Nina said. "Apparently all these Jewish husbands took off like shots. Mark was just a throwback, I guess."

"He disappeared right before Thanksgiving. And around Christmastime, they found him dead." Ida was starting to sound pretty upset. One of her mother's best friends had just died, Nina reminded herself. She regretted sounding so glib.

"How did he die?" Nina asked, in what she hoped was a more respectful tone.

"He had been in some sort of a car accident. Helen was

already pretty sick, but this really worsened her condition. As I've said, she and Mark had their differences, but she had always been crazy about him, deep down."

"Did they have a funeral for him?"

"No. Helen went into the hospital the day after he died. Beverly decided to skip the funeral. And Mark had wanted to be cremated. According to his wife, anyway. So Helen never really got a chance to say good-bye to Mark."

"That couldn't have helped her condition."

"No, she just got worse and worse and after about six weeks she died. I still feel that if it hadn't been for this, she might have recovered. But who knows?"

The risotto was done. Undoubtedly Ida's nails were filed. It was time to get off the phone. "All this must be rough for you, Ma. How are you doing?"

"I'm sad. Helen and I had been friends for fifty years."

"Is there anything I can do?"

"No, I'll be okay. I'm going to spend the weekend at Esther's. She has tickets to some sort of New Jersey symphony thing." Ida and her friends often went off to spend a few days here and there, as if they were all part of some modern-day *alter kocker* Bloomsbury group. But instead of private incomes they had New York City schoolteachers' pensions. And instead of having sex with each other, they ate cake into the night.

"Well, I'm going to call Beverly now, to find out if she has a copy of Helen's will."

"Good luck with that woman," Ida said. "I never trusted her."

"Come on, you're just prejudiced against women who wear high heels. You should be more open-minded."

"Why?" asked Ida.

Nina couldn't think of an answer.

4 . . . .

Nina dialed Beverly Hirsch's number at five o'clock on Monday afternoon. Five o'clock was the time of day when all the real phone calls got made in law offices. Calls made between nine and five were merely obligatory gestures, never meant to result in climax. They fell into the category of "I'm returning your call because I'm forced to" or "I have to call you for some reason or another, but I'd be willing to wait another day or two on this."

Lawyers never actually reached each other before five. If you called another lawyer at nine, they weren't in yet. By ten, they had "stepped away from their desk," probably to the coffee room, or the bathroom, or they were frantically looking to see who had grabbed that day's *Law Journal*. Or they were in a colleague's office, discussing sports, or relationships, or gossiping about each other. In any event, they hadn't settled in yet and were not available to take calls. And by eleven, they were bound to be in a meeting that would last until lunch.

Lunch generally commenced by one-thirty, although lunches had been known to take place much later. Among lawyers there was this strange shibboleth that the later you ate, the cooler you were—like college students who had spent their junior year in Barcelona and came home to snootily inform their parents that they couldn't even *think* about dinner before ten. Lawyers liked to pretend that they were so involved in their work, they could hardly tear themselves away for lunch.

They'd be back by three, but would have to spend the afternoon hours taking phone calls from clients. Paying clients, that is. So if opposing counsel or any other type of non-client called anytime before five, they were more than likely to have to leave a message with a secretary who insisted that her boss was on another call.

But after five, when the secretary packed up and went home, lawyers had to answer their own phones. And you could actually get through. Most lawyers spent the hours between five and seven talking to each other on the phone. All actual legal work, such as drafting papers or reviewing documents, was done on the Metro-North train in and out of Grand Central.

Nina really intended to talk to Beverly. She knew she had damn well better get a copy of Helen's will soon, even though she dreaded her role as executor. So she called her at five, the time she was used to actually reaching someone on the phone. What she forgot was that the suburban housewife operates on a schedule different from the New York City lawyer.

The worst time to try to reach a housewife at home, at least one of the Beverly Hirsch variety, is five o'clock in the afternoon. They're generally in during the mornings, when their children and husband and all other disruptive characters have departed, leaving them to their coffee and quiet.

And then they might actually do some housework. Tolerance for this varies, but generally does not exceed forty-five minutes. In Beverly's case, Nina suspected that the entire concept of keeping house had been dispensed with.

The tedium of cleaning is often relieved by the telephone, a phase that can last quite some time. By mid-afternoon, after having worked their way through most of a six-pack of English muffins, and with their kids almost on their way home from school, it's time to get out of the house. The rest of the day is divided between the gym, the mall, and finally the take-out shop. They exhaustedly stagger home at the last minute before dinner and drop their containers of food onto the dining room table.

Because they're damned if they're going to cook. Cooking in this day and age is generally performed by underpaid immigrants in the food service industry or by recently divorced men taking courses. Women like Beverly remain haunted by images of their own mothers, shoulders hunched and stomachs sticking out, cutting cucumbers over the sink. And they're not going to let that happen to them. They don't do weight training three times a week and take daily calcium supplements to combat osteoporosis, just so that their posture can be ruined by a goddamn vegetable. So the family only eats cucumbers on the nights when Mom has picked up a pound of Greek salad from the deli.

Of course, there are variations on this routine. Some women sit around in their bathrobes and drink. Others have affairs. Some suburban women actually spend their afternoons doing their own gardening. Not in Great Neck, of course, but in some of the blue-blooded communities, gardening actually consumes the better part of the day.

Beverly Hirsch, however, did not do her own gardening. She liked to shop, but she did not consider a flat of impatiens or an azalea bush to be a consumer item. These were things meant to be sold to the trade only. Besides, there was the fingernail problem.

Nina had watched enough prime-time television to be able to figure out that Beverly would not be home at this hour. But she just wasn't thinking. Her intentions were honest. She never meant to reach Lisa.

"Is your mom there?" Nina asked.

"No, she's not in. Can I take a message?"

"It's Nina Fischman. Can you have her—"

"Oh, I know who you are. You were looking for a copy of my grandmother's will. I found it for you."

"Really? That was fast. Do you want a job as my secretary?"

"Well, it was really no problem. I'm familiar with my father's files. I figured it would be there."

The kid had a great phone voice. You'd think she were a polished, highly confident executive, rather than a chubby adolescent who kept tugging at her sweater to make sure it didn't catch in the back of her waistband.

"Could you send me a copy?"

"Absolutely. By the way, he also had a file with lists of all of my grandmother's assets. Like where her safe-deposit box is and stuff like that. Would you like a copy of that also?"

"That would be really helpful. By the way, what did the will say? If you've read it, that is."

"Of course I've read it. It's simple. Everything goes to my father if he's still alive. And to me if he's not. And it names him as the executor and you as the alternate."

"Yeah, that I remember. By the way, when exactly did your father die? If you don't mind my asking. I'll probably need to know."

"Why did he die?"

"No, when did he die? He died in a car accident, right?"

Lisa mumbled something inaudible. "What did you say?" Nina asked.

"Nothing. Never mind. You know what I think I should do? Send you a copy of his death certificate. You might need it."

"Thanks, I might. I'm not really sure what I'll need. I've never done this before."

"I'm sure you'll figure it out." Which one was the adolescent here, anyway? Nina started to wonder.

"How have things been since your father died?" Nina asked. She knew it was too intimate a question under the circumstances. But it was sometimes that way with women. Even fifteen-year-olds. She'd find herself embarking on very intimate conversations even without a preexisting relationship. Nina would start talking to some woman at a party and after a few sentences, the conversation might take a turn toward the personal.

It didn't happen with all women, of course. Just a certain kind. It was like meeting a man and immediately finding your capillaries dilating and all of a sudden you're flirting and saying all sorts of things that would sound very embarrassing if anyone ever played back a tape of the conversation. With women it was different, but also the same in a way.

Nina felt that tug of intimacy toward Lisa, despite her age. The child must have felt it, too, because unlike most monosyllabic teenagers, she launched into a rather revealing response.

"Not great. But then, things weren't great even when he was alive. We were never the perfect American family."

"Who is?"

"Yeah, but it's hard not to believe we were worse than most. My mother always fought with both me and my father. It got really bad in the past couple of years, I think, when he stopped making money. He was always in a lousy mood, worrying about business. And she would get really hysterical about not being able to pay the bills and all."

"It sounds bad."

"Yeah, at the time I thought it couldn't get much worse. But when my father disappeared and I was left alone with her . . . well, I thought that I just might not be able to survive. I hadn't realized how much of a buffer he was. The whole time he was missing, I kept telling myself that he would come back, that this wouldn't last forever. But he didn't. And it has."

"It must have been terrible."

"It was. The funny thing was that Mom got a little better after we found out that he was dead. Maybe she felt sorry for me and decided to lighten up."

The kid sounded so mature, Nina thought. She was probably the kind of child who's good with adults, but doesn't have any friends until she's thirty, when everyone finally decides she's really terrific. Nina hoped that Lisa would make it to thirty without too much damage. Knowing that everyone else's mother really likes you is not necessarily enough to get you through adolescence.

"Do you miss your grandmother?" Helen Hirsch might have been responsible for cultivating this mature streak in Lisa. Nina would bet it had little to do with Beverly.

"She was the only one I could really talk to. It sounds corny, but it's true." It was nice that this next generation could actually relate to their grandparents. These days grandparents not only spoke English but wore sweat suits and running shoes. Nina's grandmother had worn Cuban heels and a girdle. And spoke limited English, mostly consisting of pejorative adjectives.

"I hope that things settle down over there," Nina said. "If there's anything I or my mother can do, let us know. My mother was very fond of Helen. She really misses her."

"That's very nice of you. Maybe there'll be enough money in Grandma's will to send me to boarding school."

"Are you serious? Is that what you want?"

"I don't know. I might miss my dog."

Lisa was only a kid, Nina reminded herself. And it was not helpful to pretend that she wasn't, that the usual rules for fifteen-year-olds didn't apply. Nina had always hated that bullshit about being held to a higher standard. She had hated it when she was fifteen and she shouldn't lay it on Lisa now.

"I'll call your mother and arrange to get the documents. When's a good time to get her?"

"These days it's hard to say. She's been getting around a lot lately."

"What do you mean by that?" As soon as she asked, she regretted it. She sensed that she had gone too far.

"Oh, I don't know."

"I see. Well, I'll try her around nine. And thanks for your help."

"No problem," Lisa said, sounding like she had nothing but problems.

5 . . . .

The primary duty of an executor is to preserve the assets of
the estate. Most people know that, whether or not they've
gone to law school. But the implications were just starting to
sink in. It meant that Nina had to arrange to have Helen's
apartment cleaned out and vacated as soon as possible. It was
a rental, and it was Nina's duty as executor not to waste
money on rent, month after month, while the contents of the
apartment hung around, waiting to be distributed. Ideally,
she should have arranged to give up the apartment by the
end of the month. But February was such a short month. She
felt very rushed.

Nina called Beverly back later that night and this time
she was in. "It's Nina, Ida Fischman's daughter," she said.

"Hello," Beverly said coolly.

"We need to do a few things. Do you have the keys to
Helen's apartment?"

"They're somewhere. I can find them."

"I'm going to have to see to it that the apartment is vacated soon. Would you meet me there so that we can go through Helen's stuff and figure out what to do with it?"

"I guess so." Still cool.

"When's good for you?" Nina asked.

"Tomorrow's okay. Around three in the afternoon?"

"Okay." Nina had a ton of work on her desk. But then, she always had a ton of work on her desk. "How do I get there?"

"Take the E or F train to Continental Avenue. Do you know your way around that subway station?"

"Not really." Nina was an IRT woman. The E and F were mysterious lines, whisking home scores of Chinese, Korean, and Indian commuters to unknown ethnic parts of Queens every night.

Beverly gave her specific directions to Helen's apartment. "Anything else you need?" she asked Nina.

"Could you bring a copy of Helen's will with you? I might as well get started on probating it."

"I'll try to remember," Beverly said, in a way that made clear that remembering was not her long suit.

The next day, Nina set aside an extra half hour for getting lost in Queens. It wasn't a borough that she had a great command of. But as it turned out, Helen's building was easy to find. Queens addresses began with the number of the cross street. A sensible method. Not like the Bronx, where almost every street had a name and a hundred emotional connotations.

The building on Queens Boulevard was undistinctive. A white brick, postwar high-rise, it featured concrete balconies with frosted glass panels. The lobby was utilitarian and empty, probably deliberately Spartan to discourage loitering. These buildings didn't hold a candle to the prewar grandeur of the Grand Concourse. But if you were an old Jewish lady, you'd probably rather be walking down Queens Boulevard than the Grand Concourse these days. The architecture was the least of it.

Nina waited in the lobby, leaning against the mailbox wall, for at least fifteen minutes. The Hirsches finally appeared, Beverly tottering on high heels and frantically rummaging through her purse. Shit, Nina thought, she forgot the key to Helen's apartment. *Why am I not surprised?* But Beverly finally dug it out, after much eye-rolling from her daughter. Lisa handed Nina an envelope, presumably containing the will.

In the elevator on the way up, Nina snuck a peek at it. The will said pretty much what Lisa had recounted. The only unusual provision was that the trustee for Lisa, in the event that Mark predeceased Helen, was a bank officer. It would have been more usual to name Beverly as trustee. It was odd, Nina thought. Well, maybe not odd as much as insulting.

Beverly fumbled with the locks a bit, gingerly enough to avoid doing any damage to her nails. When the door finally swung open, Nina was struck by how similar Helen's home was to Ida's apartment. It could have been done by the same decorator, had Helen and Ida been women who were prone to hiring decorators. The ethnic artifacts and aging Danish modern furniture were, Nina supposed, de rigueur among Hunter women of a certain age.

Lisa went right over to the living room couch, propped a pillow up against a teak arm, and lay down. She immediately picked up the remote control and commenced a furiously brisk channel scan that went on for about ten minutes. She finally settled on *Wall Street Week*. Definitely a strange kid, Nina thought.

In the meantime, Beverly walked around and surveyed the contents of the apartment. Nina soon got the drift that there wasn't going to be much arguing about Helen's things. Nineteen fifty-eight might have been a banner year for

Dansk, but Beverly wasn't interested. "Let me know if you want anything," she said to Nina. "Otherwise it's all going to cousin Alan."

"Who's cousin Alan?"

"A nerd," Lisa shouted from the couch. "His wife finally threw him out and now he's sleeping on a cot in a studio apartment in Bayside."

When they got to the kitchen, Beverly made a beeline for a set of Limoges dessert plates, which she quickly wrapped in newspaper. "I think there's some Lalique somewhere," she said, rummaging around in the back of a cabinet.

"You might have imagined it," Lisa said, joining them. "My mother hallucinates Lalique."

Beverly finally gave up on the Lalique and wandered toward the bedroom. She gave a rather desultory poke through Helen's jewelry box. It contained mostly rhinestones and Mexican silver, which she threw into a shopping bag to be sorted through later.

Nobody really got going until Beverly opened the double folding closet door in Helen's bedroom and let out a whoop. "Look at this," she called, and Lisa and Nina rushed down the hall to see. "The woman never threw anything out." From Beverly's perfectly manicured right hand hung a garment that appeared to be a dress. Or at least three-quarters of a dress; its actual length could not have exceeded twenty-eight inches. It had no discernible waist and was decorated with rectangles of primary colors.

"Mondrian," Beverly and Nina said simultaneously. They both giggled.

"What?" said Lisa.

"I didn't know that my mother-in-law was such a fashion plate," Beverly continued. "Let's see if she has little white go-go boots to go with the dress."

"Courrèges," Nina said.

"Right," Beverly said. "Which one of us is going to try this on?" she asked, swinging the dress in front of her.

"Not me," Nina said. "It didn't work for me the first time around, and I'm certainly not going to put myself through that again." Nina was always trying to make her long skirts look fashionable, but sometimes she felt like a member of a religious sect. As soon as she had successfully convinced herself that she was simply a well-dressed person who marched to a different drummer, the lady behind the bakery counter would speak Yiddish to her. Or some bewigged woman would stop her in the street, only to shrug apologetically and explain that she had mistaken her for someone named Rifka.

But she didn't have much choice. "I'll leave the short skirts to you," she told Beverly.

"You're no fun." Beverly pouted. "All that sixties stuff is back. This is a real collector's item. Lisa, want to try it on? It'll look adorable on you."

Lisa examined the garment cautiously. She ran her fingers over the black lines that divided the red and blue rectangles. "It's neat," she said. "But I don't know if—"

"Try it," her mother snapped.

"No." Lisa's lower lip began to tremble.

"Okay, okay," Beverly said. "I'll try it on." She flung the dress onto the bed and pulled off her oversize sweater, careful not to dislodge the rhinestone bows. Then she slipped the dress on over her black spandex leggings. Those ubiquitous black spandex leggings. They seemed to have become a badge of honor among suburban women, the housedress of the nineties. It had taken a while for Nina to stop thinking that everyone had forgotten to put on their pants.

Beverly changed clothes quickly, but Nina had enough time to notice a lacy black bra, which covered little more than the bottom half of her breasts. "What do you think?" Beverly crossed the room and stood in front of the full-length mirror.

"Not bad for an old lady, huh?" The latter was directed at Lisa.

"Great, Ma," Lisa said.

"We used to wear these things with fishnet stockings," she said, running a hand up her own thigh, "and those go-go boots and the tiniest little pocketbooks. And white lipstick." Beverly traced the outline of her lips with a red fingernail. "And, of course, we all wore those hairpieces. Falls. Did you have a fall, Nina?"

"No."

Beverly turned to Lisa. "We'd wear our falls with those wide cloth headbands. I guess they called them falls because they fell halfway down our backs." She lifted her big black hair up with her hands, à la Brigitte Bardot, and then let it cascade back down. She was clearly a woman who enjoyed touching herself. "Such fun times, weren't they, Nina?"

"I guess so."

"I had such a lovely figure back then."

Nina knew she had an obligation to say "but you still look wonderful," so she did.

"But after childbirth, the waist is never the same." She flattened the dress against her abdomen and then punched herself lightly in the gut. "I'm strong, but definitely thicker. Compared to what I was."

Nina looked over to Lisa, who had taken on the guilty look of a culprit. "Now, Nina," Beverly went on, "you still have such a nice small waist." She pretended to be looking at Nina's waist, but it was obvious that she was really sneaking a look at Nina's rear end.

Nina gave her what she wanted. "My waist is only small in comparison to my hips."

"You know there are things you can do," Beverly said, now staring unabashedly at Nina's thighs.

"Spare me," Nina said. "I've done more leg lifts in my life than Jack LaLanne and Jane Fonda combined."

"I'm not talking leg lifts," Beverly said as she folded the Mondrian dress neatly and put it into a shopping bag.

Nina felt that if she heard this thin woman in a black bra and leggings utter the word liposuction, she would run out of the room screaming. To distract Beverly, Nina dived into the closet and retrieved a red silk Chinese bathrobe. "Here's something that might fit one of us," she said to Lisa. "Want to try it on?"

The child brightened visibly and within thirty seconds was doing a credible imitation of her mother, posing in front of the mirror and running her hand up and down the sides of her silk-covered body.

The afternoon proceeded, with Beverly trying on all of Helen's old dresses and Lisa trying on the coats, robes, and shoes. Mother and daughter vied for mirror space. Nina meanwhile began boxing things up, then gave cousin Alan a call to make arrangements. He wasn't in, but the message on his machine didn't sound too bad.

Maybe she should investigate cousin Alan further. Everyone said the newly separated ones made the best prospects. The sooner you got to them the better, just off the vine and all that. She beat back the image of fresh dogshit on a cold winter morning, still steaming slightly from the warmth of a canine bowel. Lisa had said he was a nerd, not a turd. What an attitude Nina had.

After mother and daughter finally tore themselves away from the mirror, they all schlepped a bunch of stuff down to Beverly's red Toyota Celica. It was a sexy car, curvy in the right places. Beverly had a miniature pair of aerobics shoes hanging from the rearview mirror.

Nina went back upstairs and flipped open the envelope that Lisa had given her. Underneath the will was Mark's death certificate. He had died in Lake Placid, New York, on December 20th. Attached to the death certificate was a copy of the Lake Placid police department's accident report. She probably wouldn't need this, but she took a look. According to the report, Mark drove himself off the road at eleven-thirty at night. There was no other car involved. The road was clear of ice. And he had been intoxicated.

Nina wondered about Mark. She wasn't surprised that the sexy juvenile delinquent she remembered had ended up driving himself drunkenly to his death. He seemed destined to live fast. But she wondered what he had been doing up in Lake Placid. She supposed it was true that the Beverly and Lisa show might be enough to drive a man to making a few stops on his way home from work. But was it enough to drive him into hiding? Even with a sinking business and a mother dying of cancer, why drop out of sight?

Nina tried to picture Mark Hirsch's life. Lisa had said that her parents fought a lot. Maybe that had something to do with Mark's drinking. How bad a problem had it been? She reached for Helen's phone, an old black table model, reminding herself that it was her responsibility as executor to discontinue service as soon as possible.

"Hello?" Ida was in.

"Ma, it's me."

"Home from the wars?"

"Not yet, I'm still at Helen's."

"How did it go?"

"It was fairly grotesque. Beverly summarily rejected almost everything, except for a set of dishes that she obviously had her eye on for years. And some old clothes that she said were back in fashion. Stuff from the sixties. Pretty racy stuff for Helen. I never pictured her in minidresses."

"She went through an obsessive Weight Watchers phase and actually reached goal, as they say in the biz. So she ran out and bought a whole new wardrobe. She outgrew it in a few months, of course. But I guess she could never bear to throw it out."

"Of course not," Nina said. "Our fat clothes, which we fit into ninety percent of the time, we have no trouble throwing out at the drop of a hat. As soon as we lose five pounds and the size fourteen gets the tiniest bit baggy, it's time for the Salvation Army. But the stuff we can only squeeze into for a couple of weeks out of our entire lives gets dragged around with us for decades."

"Maybe those clothes remind us of the good times. The thin times."

"Mother, being thin is very enjoyable and I'm glad that I've gotten to experience it a few times in my life. But as far as I'm concerned, it's like traveling in a foreign country. I mean, Paris is a beautiful city, but I don't expect to live there."

"Why not?"

"I don't speak French. Anyway, that's not why I called. I was curious about something. I wanted to know how bad a drinking problem Mark Hirsch had."

"Problem? What do you mean by problem?"

"Would you say that he was an alcoholic?"

"Not at all," Ida said. "Mark had a problem with alcohol, but it wasn't a drinking problem in the conventional sense."

"What do you mean?"

"Mark didn't drink. He couldn't drink. He had been a diabetic since high school. A severe one. He couldn't tolerate alcohol at all. I remember he got drunk once as an adolescent and almost went into a coma. After that he was very careful. Not only about alcohol, but about everything he put in his mouth. He was scrupulous."

"That doesn't make sense. I have the accident report from the Lake Placid police and it says he was intoxicated when he drove himself off the road. I don't get it."

"Maybe the police made a mistake," Ida said. "Or maybe they're covering something up."

"Or maybe someone killed him and then staged a drunk driving accident."

"Well, if someone did that," Ida said, "I'll bet I know who it was."

"Let me guess. Beverly."

"Right."

"Ma, just because the woman wears high heels doesn't mean she murdered her husband. Although I must say, wearing high heels to clean out your dead mother-in-law's apartment did strike me as pretty stupid."

"I bet you had to carry all the boxes."

"Wrong. Lisa and I shared them."

"Figures."

"Maybe we shouldn't be so judgmental," Nina said. "There are some women who *have* to wear high heels. They start out wearing them young and then they wear them so much that the tendons in the back of their calves shrink and they can't wear flats anymore."

"Not Beverly. After all, she told you at the funeral that aerobics was her life. Do you think she goes to class in her black lizard pumps?"

"I guess not, but . . . seriously, I think we have a very puzzling situation here. The whole thing smells. I have to think about this."

"Think about it," Ida said. "But don't rule her out."

6 . . . .

She had to talk to Beverly about this. The conversation was one that Nina would rather have in person, but when was she going to get back out to Great Neck? The Long Island Rail Road was a waste of time. She supposed she could borrow her brother-in-law's car, but getting to Brooklyn was a pain in and of itself. Usually, being carless was no problem. She rode her little circuit, circumscribed by wherever the IRT could take her. But suddenly, her circuit seemed to have taken a giant detour eastward.

Nina decided to go out there right now. What the hell, Queens Boulevard was already halfway there. She checked her purse for cash. Amazingly, there was fifty bucks in there. She was usually lucky to find a ten. New Yorkers dealt with their cash supply the way they did their marketing, with a nightly stop on the way home from work for just enough to get them through the next day. They lived in a world without wads of bills or grocery carts.

She looked around the apartment and found Helen's address book on a table in the foyer. First she dialed Beverly, but there was no answer. Maybe she and Lisa were stuck in traffic. Well, they'd be back eventually, wouldn't they? There was no listing under *T* for taxi, but she found one under *C* for car service. Nina called the number and a man picked up. "Haifa," he said, with an accent.

"I'm on Queens Boulevard and I need to get to twenty-five Executive Drive in Manhasset Hills," she said, reading from Helen's book. "It's somewhere near Great Neck. Do you know where it is? Because I certainly don't."

"Sure, no problem." Nina couldn't be sure whether she should believe him. Israelis always sounded so cocky, it was hard to imagine they were Jews. They never used words like "maybe" or "possibly" or "ambivalent."

"How much is this going to cost?"

"Twenty-three dollars."

"Okay." She'd worry about getting home later. Nina gave him Helen's address. "I'll be in front of the building. How soon can you get here?"

"Five minutes." Again, Nina couldn't tell if he meant it or not. She rushed down to the lobby and a car appeared about ten minutes later.

The driver was adorable, with blue eyes and dark curly hair. Nina idly wondered if it was too late for her to go through an Israeli-men phase. She had friends who had, but they had done it while they were in their twenties. Like her friends who had gone through their Mexican-men phase. Both the Israeli and Mexican men had proved problematic, but the women all had fabulous silver jewelry to show for it.

In addition to being cute, the driver seemed to know where he was going. He headed east on the Long Island Expressway, then guided them south onto Lakeville Road. Then started making lefts and rights with authority. "Can I ask you something, since you seem to know the area," Nina said. "Is Manhasset Hills actually part of Great Neck?"

"Well, yes and no. You see, Great Neck is made up of separate villages—Great Neck Estates, Great Neck Plaza, Kings Point, Kensington, like that. The village of Great Neck itself is very small. So maybe you could get away with counting Manhasset Hills in there. Especially since it's right near the high school. Great Neck South, that is."

"So is Manhasset Hills expensive?" Nina asked.

"Not compared to the neighborhoods farther north. I would say that in general, the farther north you go, the fancier the neighborhood."

"Do you live around there?"

"Me? I live in Queens."

"So how come you know so much about the area?"

"How come?" He shrugged adorably. "Great Neck is the promised land."

Nina noticed the adorable shrug, and then noticed that they had turned onto Executive Drive. And there was Beverly's red Toyota Celica, parked in the driveway of a white split-level. She gave the driver twenty-three dollars, plus another seven for cuteness, and marched up to Beverly's door. The dog started barking and someone called "Who is it?" before she even got a chance to ring the bell.

That was the creepy thing about the suburbs. People became aware of your presence before you wanted them to. In the city, visitors had to get past doormen and intercom systems and elevators and multiple locks, all of which gave you time to adjust to the idea of sharing space with another person.

"It's Nina," she shouted, over the dog.

Beverly came to the door. She was still wearing her high heels. Maybe she did have a tendon problem.

"This is a surprise." Beverly sounded more annoyed

than surprised. The dog, a small white fluffy thing, yapped around her high heels.

"I've got to talk to you about something."

"Well, come in." Beverly led her into the living room. To the left, down a few stairs, a television rumbled, presumably in the den. The dog followed them into the living room, but before its little toes hit the white rug, Beverly yelled for Lisa.

"What?" Lisa's voice came from the den.

"Get Bunny out of the living room," Beverly shouted. "Off the rug," she ordered the dog.

Lisa came in and swooped Bunny up. "What are you doing here?" she asked Nina.

"There's a matter I have to discuss with your mother."

"Really?" Lisa said, stepping off the rug into the entry-way. "About what?"

"I think we better make this a private discussion," Nina said.

"Why don't you and Bunny go upstairs?" Beverly said. Lisa looked troubled, but headed for her bedroom. "Now, would you like something to drink?"

"Diet Coke?" Nina never drank the stuff, but there was something about the Hirsch residence that cried out for it. She'd put money on it being the house beverage. As Beverly took off for the kitchen, Nina looked around. The living room could have been a museum exhibit entitled "The Nadir of Modern Design." An ugly, quilted three-dimensional "painting" hung on the wall over the couch. The white car-peting had black and peach zigzags sewn into it. A huge black lacquer and smoked-glass wall unit featured a collection of marble eggs and Lladró porcelain figures. Beverly returned with soda in a heavy glass tumbler.

"What's the problem?" Beverly settled into the peach-colored leather modular couch.

"I was just taking a look at the documents you brought

me. Helen's will and Mark's death certificate and the accident report."

"Did we give you a copy of the accident report?" Beverly went from looking annoyed to looking alert. Her eyes involuntarily flickered up toward Lisa's bedroom.

"Yes, you did. Beverly, did Mark have a drinking problem?"

"No, not really."

"What do you mean, not really?"

"Well, you know . . . I wouldn't really say . . . he didn't actually . . ." Beverly stumbled around until Nina cut her off.

When in doubt, cross-examine. "Isn't it true that he never drank? That he was a severe diabetic who couldn't touch alcohol?"

Beverly was quiet for a moment. "That's true," she finally said.

"So why did the accident report say that he was intoxicated?"

"I don't know." Beverly looked at the floor.

"Did you see the accident report?"

"Of course."

"Weren't you disturbed by the discrepancy?"

"Sure." She was still looking at the floor.

"Didn't you mention it to anyone?"

"No."

"Why not?"

Beverly breathed in and out a few times, puffily, as if she were doing abdominal exercises. Her eyes narrowed and she finally lifted them from the floor. She stared at Nina proudly, like a child who has just lit upon the right answer in class. "Suicide," she said. "I was afraid that his death might be considered suicide. And that would mean that I could be disqualified from collecting on his life insurance policy. Which, believe me, I need. It's all he left me."

"But what makes you think it was suicide?"

"For Mark, drinking was suicidal."

"But why then drive himself off the road?" Nina asked. "If he was going to drive himself off the road anyway, why get drunk first? What was the point? And if alcohol had such a severe effect on him, would he even have been able to drive at all?"

"I'm not saying he actually killed himself. All I said was that I was afraid someone would think he did and hold up the life insurance benefits. Which was why I didn't say anything about the discrepancy." Beverly leaned back on the couch, satisfied.

Nina was less than satisfied. The whole performance had the air of a child who hadn't done her homework. She had lied right off the bat about whether or not Mark drank. And this suicide business seemed like something she had come up with on the spur of the moment. Bunny barked from the top of the stairs and Nina caught a glimpse of Lisa retreating into her room. She wondered how much of the conversation the girl had heard.

"I see." Nina decided not to be too confrontational right now. She wanted to think about things. Besides, she needed a ride to the train station. "Well, I guess that makes sense."

"Is there anything else I can do for you?" Beverly asked.

"Would it be too much trouble for you to drive me over to the train station?" There seemed no point in checking the Great Neck train schedule. At the moment Nina would rather wait at the station than hang around in Beverly's living room.

Beverly looked at her watch. "Let's go right now," she said abruptly.

"Okay." Nina was relieved.

"Lisa, we're going to the station," Beverly shouted. "If Stuart gets here, tell him I'll be right back."

"Can't I come?" Lisa and Bunny ran down the stairs together.

"Someone has to be here to let Stuart in."

"But you know that I hate—"

Beverly cut her off. "Enough." She reached into the closet and pulled out a three-quarter-length mink. "My car coat," she explained to Nina, who smiled back.

"Nice," Nina said, doing what was expected of her, and stroked the coat.

As they drove down the block, a gray Mercedes headed toward them. Beverly slowed and rolled down her window. The driver of the Mercedes did the same. "Be back in a little while," Beverly told him. "Just going to the train station."

"Okay, babe," he said. Then he looked at Nina and Nina looked at him. He was tan, maybe fifty-five. He wasn't wearing a coat or gloves. Nina noticed a V-neck sweater with no shirt under it and a gold ID bracelet on the wrist that rested against the steering wheel.

Halfway down the street, she couldn't stop herself from looking over her shoulder at his car. Nina knew that Beverly would find her snooping annoying, but she was rewarded by a glimpse of his license plate, right before he turned into the driveway. It was a vanity plate with five letters. TRASH.

. . . .

7

Nina called Ida before she went to bed and described her visit with Beverly. "I really can't figure out what's going on," Nina said. "She lied at first when I asked about Mark's drinking. And then she came up with that suicide crap. Plus she has a boyfriend who looks as if he bathes people in concrete for a living."

"Don't jump to any conclusions until you talk to Lisa. She's only fifteen, but she's got a lot on the ball."

"She certainly seems to."

"To tell you the truth, I think that if it weren't for her grandchild, Helen would have cashed in her chips when she was originally diagnosed three years ago. She lived for that child."

"How come?"

"Well, after Jack died, Lisa was the only one Helen could really relate to. Mark and Beverly made her nervous, with their screaming and the jewelry and the Las Vegas vacations. She didn't really have that much use for them."

"So she made her granddaughter over in her own image?"

"Not completely. It's not always so easy," Ida said.

Nina thought about her niece Danielle, who always managed to convince her grandmother to buy her a new outfit on the way to whichever museum Ida was dragging her to. "Lisa seems more of a hybrid to me," Nina said. "She certainly got into trying on Helen's old clothes today."

Nina still hadn't gotten around to calling Lisa by the next evening, when the phone rang. It was Lisa. Why doesn't it ever work this way with men, Nina thought.

"What's up?" she asked.

"Can you come out here? Sometime when my mother won't be home. I'd like to talk to you. Alone. About my father."

"I guess so," Nina said. Yet another schlep on the Long Island Rail Road. Maybe she should consider getting a commuter ticket until things calmed down. "Can we meet somewhere near the train station? I don't have a car."

"Can't you borrow one?"

Nina considered explaining how the nearest car she knew was an hour away by subway in Brooklyn. It would sound too bizarre to a suburban teenager. It certainly wouldn't get her any points for coolness. "It's easier for me to take the train," Nina said. "Isn't there someplace convenient where we could go for ice cream or something?"

"Good idea. We can go to Bruce's. You can walk there and I can ride my bike over. It's two blocks from the station. Right on Middle Neck Road. You can't miss it. Just ask anybody if you can't find it."

"Can it wait until Saturday?"

"If it has to," Lisa said.

After all, Nina had to go to the office sometime. All this

Hirsch business had cut into her productivity. Which hadn't been at an all-time record lately to begin with. She had been toying with the same motion papers for a week now, changing around the whereases and the therefores until it was all a blur.

By Saturday, Nina was pretty worked up. Maybe it had been a mistake to have put Lisa off. The girl seemed so fragile. What if she had really needed to talk to Nina and irreparable harm had been done by waiting?

Bruce's was easy to find. She followed the crowd over the railway trestle to the north side of the station. Then she quite naturally drifted west, somehow sensing that was where the action was. And it was. Middle Neck Road, despite the cold weather, was a bustle of activity. Shearling seemed to be the Saturday morning wrap of preference. Not the kind people used to wear, not the orangy-tan kind with little white tufts sticking out between the seams. But the new, improved kind that Searle made, all sculpted down so that it looked like suede, dyed sedate colors like dark purple and bottle-green.

The restaurant was right past a couple of fancy boutiques. Nina, however, was not prepared for the cultural oddities she found there. Lisa was late, so she had time to observe the natives, who were all busy table-hopping. They were loud and gregarious and everyone seemed to know everyone else. It was like one of those nightclub scenes in a forties movie. But instead of wearing dinner jackets and evening gowns, husbands and wives all wore running suits. The women's were festooned with various types of ornamentation. Rhinestones were popular, as were buttons, bows, beads, and feathers. One woman wore a sweater decorated with rows of bullets.

There seemed to be a ritual to eating at Bruce's. On each table sat two baskets, one with rolls and one with pastries. The women, after ordering half a cantaloupe, dived into a basket, usually working their way from the rolls to the pastries. It was the worst kind of food sexism, Nina told herself. But she had always been one to experience local customs firsthand. Nina commenced to do some damage to her own pastry basket.

Finally Lisa arrived. She wore an outfit that was a curious mix of Great Neck and the Lower East Side—a North Shore beaded sweater, accessorized with black combat boots and a beat-up army jacket.

Lisa perused the menu nervously, changing her mind several times. Finally, she settled on a croissant topped with chocolate frozen yogurt. A disgusting combination, Nina thought. But she was hardly a food purist, having mixed and matched many culinary items that would make most people retch. Salami and jelly sandwiches had been a favorite for a while. Later, during the marijuana years, it had been all the rage at the student union to put honey on your French fries. And there had been a chicken mole period, when chocolate had been poured over poultry in all sorts of inappropriate ways. But she wouldn't expect anyone to put these dishes on a menu. She decided to stick with the pastry basket and just ordered coffee.

She let Lisa settle into her frozen yogurt before she launched in. "What was it you wanted to discuss?"

"There are a lot of things my mother didn't tell you about my father."

"Like what?"

"Like he was supposed to be missing, but she knew where he was. And like the reason he disappeared was because he was afraid of being killed."

"Really. Why don't you start at the beginning," Nina said gently. "Tell me whatever you think is important."

"Well, before he disappeared he told me that he was going out of town. That he couldn't go into details, but he felt it would be better if he dropped out of sight for a while. And that he couldn't tell me or anyone else where he was going. It wasn't because he didn't trust me. But if I knew where he was, then someone might try to force me to tell them and I could get hurt."

"But he told your mother where he was going?"

"Absolutely not. If he didn't tell me, he wasn't about to tell *her*."

"But you said she knew where he was."

"Not at first. He disappeared without saying anything to her. He didn't even tell her what he told me," Lisa said proudly. "And boy, was she pissed. She kept screaming about all the bills he left her with, and that there was nothing in the bank account and how rotten he was."

"What did she do about the bills?"

"Well, it's my private opinion that she got that creep Stuart Grossman to help her out. Because he appeared on the scene pretty soon after Daddy disappeared. Too soon, if you ask me."

"Is that the guy who drives the gray Mercedes? With the license plate that says TRASH?"

"Yeah, that old guy."

"Why does he have that on his license plate anyway?"

"He owns some company that hauls away garbage. He and that disgusting partner of his, Mr. Maggio, who practically molests me every time he comes over. They're both trash as far as I'm concerned."

"So how did your mother figure out where your father was?"

"She hired some private detective to find him."

"And he found him?"

"Oh, yeah, he found him all right. But by that time, I don't think my mother was so thrilled about him being found. Stuart the Gross Man was around almost all the time, and she had big new diamond earrings."

Lisa definitely sounded less like the highly confident polished executive of the previous week. "Where did your father turn up?"

"In a town upstate. Lake Placid."

"What was he doing there?"

"Selling condo units in a ski resort. I guess he still had to make a living. And he had a New York real estate broker's license, so it made sense."

"How do you know all this, if I may ask?"

"Just by hanging out at the top of the stairs." Lisa finished off her frozen yogurt, picked up her empty bowl, and gave it a lick. "Excuse me, I've got to go to the bathroom."

Nina laid waste to a couple of mini-Danishes while she waited. When Lisa returned, her eyes looked red and swollen. Maybe Nina had been pumping her too hard. She didn't want to get the kid hysterical. But she did have a wealth of information. "Are you all right?"

"I'm fine," Lisa said fiercely.

And suddenly Nina realized that Lisa's eyes weren't red and swollen from crying. They were red and swollen from sticking her fingers down her throat and throwing up. Nina couldn't exactly tell how she knew. She just knew.

"Anyway," Lisa continued, "after the private detective found my father, Mom didn't contact him or anything. Which was more convenient as far as she was concerned. But it didn't exactly do wonders for my mental health. I thought about going up there and finding him myself, but before I knew it, the police called to tell us that he was dead."

"Did you read the accident report?" Nina asked her. She supposed there was no point in treating her with kid gloves now. The kid had already taken off on a self-induced vomiting session. Nothing worse could happen.

"Of course I did," Lisa snapped. "That stuff about his being drunk. It's all crap. Everyone knew that my father never drank. He was a diabetic and a complete fanatic about everything he put into his mouth." Suddenly Lisa's eating disorder made sense. With a weight-obsessed mother like Beverly and a compulsive diabetic father, the kid didn't have a chance.

"So what do you think happened?" Nina asked.

"He was murdered. That much I'm sure of."

"And you want me to . . ."

"Find out who did it," Lisa yelled at the top of her lungs. The woman at the next table put down her onion roll and stared. "Why do you think I gave you the accident report? And called you to meet me? Because I wanted free ice cream?"

"Lisa Hirsch, you're certainly a funny child."

"Yeah," sneered Lisa. "So funny I forgot to laugh."

8 . . . .

They had found Mark in the town of Lake Placid. It was not totally unfamiliar territory to Nina. She had never been there, but she had heard enough about the place. Tom Wilson had grown up there. And during the years that Nina had known him, they had exchanged detailed stories about their respective childhoods. They each had the ability, as listeners, to make the other one feel as though they were telling about a marvelous, exotic past.

Tom had gone back to Lake Placid to practice law, and as far as she knew, was still there. Perhaps she should call him. Maybe take a trip up there. After all, wasn't the scene of the crime the obvious place to begin an investigation? If there had been a crime, that is.

She thought about it on the train home from Great Neck. Did she or did she not want to see Tom Wilson? She couldn't decide. She always had wildly conflicting feelings about him. Maybe he didn't even live there anymore. Then the issue would be moot. Last time she had seen him, everything was status quo. His local law practice and his marriage were still ongoing, though he had made it sound like the marriage might be ending. But that could have been the kind of suggestive half-truth that a married ex-lover tells you at lunch when he's in town overnight on business.

Nina checked her address book when she got home. She felt funny about dialing his home number and getting his wife. It would be even more awkward if he wasn't living there anymore. She dialed his area code, 518, then 555-1212. According to directory assistance, his office was still in Lake Placid, but his home was now in Saranac Lake. That could mean that he had actually gotten divorced and was living on his own. Or it could mean that he and his wife and kid had picked up and bought a new house in a new neighborhood, hoping to banish the demons of past marital difficulties. Or, for all she knew, he could have run off with some new woman who had lured him away to her home turf.

Nina felt as though she had to be prepared for all the possibilities before she spoke to him—because she had always felt very vulnerable around Tom Wilson. She dialed his home number.

"Hello?" He sounded distracted.

"Tom? It's Nina Fischman."

"No kidding. Are you in town?"

"Nope, I'm calling from New York."

"Too bad," he said, in a way that made her smile. And also raised her body temperature a few tenths of a degree.

"I might be coming up there. I've gotten myself involved in this strange sort of mess." She went on to tell him about Mark's car crash and the incongruous accident report. "I thought I might talk to some of your local police to try to figure out what actually went on."

"Come on up. I'll bring you over and introduce you to the chief. We went to high school together. We're not on the same side of every case, but he's a pretty good guy. Usually cooperative."

"That would be great. I'd appreciate it."

"When do you think you might get here? I'll clear my calendar." He said it so simply and sweetly, in such an out-of-town way. New Yorkers could never clear their calendars. It was always much too complicated, or at least it was important to give that impression.

"How about mid-week? What's good for you? I don't want to disrupt anything."

"You won't be. Annie's with her mom during the week."

"Oh, did you and Chris split up?"

"I thought I told you when we had lunch last year."

"You said you might be getting divorced, but I didn't know whether or not to . . . um . . ." Nina drifted off.

"Whether or not to believe it? Well, believe it." He sounded a little sharp. Well, not really sharp as much as beleaguered. "I moved to Saranac, the next town over. I was sick of seeing her everywhere I went. Besides, Placid has changed so much, I can't relate to it anymore. Condos and fast-food joints. My practice is still there, though."

"How about if I rent a car on Thursday morning and drive up? How long does it take?"

"About six hours. Can you handle that long a drive?"

"I'm out of practice, but I think I can manage it. I'll stay somewhere in Lake Placid. It'll be more, uh, convenient." She paused uncertainly.

"If that's what you want." He sounded beleaguered again. "I'll make you a reservation at the Whiteface Inn. You'll like it. They've ruined it somewhat, but not entirely. And it's easy to find. When you get to town, just ask anyone for directions. Call me at my office after you check in. We'll have dinner." Dinner. The word had more definite sexual overtones than lunch.

Nina was nervous all that week. Although considering who she was and how she lived her life, it was sometimes hard to tell. Her normal day-to-day existence was not exactly played out in a tranquility tank. But that week she was more tense than usual. For one thing, she kept waking up at four o'clock in the morning and spending hours lying in bed, making mental lists of things like how many women in her office had pierced ears and how many people she knew had children named Sarah. And how many times she had seen Tom Wilson in the past five years.

Picking up the rental car was also nerve-racking. Unlike a lot of other borough girls, Nina had an extensive past as a competent driver. Still, getting from the rental place onto the highway always involved a lot of profuse sweating. Her sunglasses would steam up and she would never feel comfortable until she had crossed the Tappan Zee Bridge. But this was considered normal behavior in New York City, a place where people were capable of amazing accomplishments, but often couldn't perform the simple task of operating a motor vehicle.

Once she was on the open road, Nina usually relaxed and had a good time. Driving was the only activity during which she got to listen to the radio anymore. She used to listen while she cooked. But these days preparing complicated meals seemed passé, a vestige of an era when people still jogged and bought Akitas. And when she did get the urge to do something like make risotto, she tried to talk on the phone at the same time.

As the landscape changed, her mood shifted. In New York City, there's really no weather. You might notice a dusting of snow or some rain as you're scuttling from the subway to the office, but mostly weather is not a tangible presence. As she headed up the New York State Thruway on a clear February morning, everything got intensely white. And it made her think about that winter weekend in New Hampshire. "Jesus," Nina said out loud, when she realized that more than a decade had passed.

Tom had always been intense. It's said that there are two kinds of trial lawyers. There are the predictable egomaniacs, who are loud and pompous and can't really follow a conversation that isn't directly about themselves. Then there are the other, more dangerous kind. Quiet to the point of detachment, at first it's hard to imagine them in the courtroom. But as litigators, they're killers, since every word is carefully crafted and aimed straight for the throat. Like Tom Wilson.

Nina didn't figure him out until halfway through their first year of law school. She had known him as a shadowy, shambling figure, seemingly incapable of coming out with anything more than "uh." So her heart sank at first when he was assigned to be her moot court partner. In a class filled with intensely verbal urban ethnics, they had matched her up with this withdrawn farm boy. But he turned out to be brilliant. She was astonished during their practice sessions when he began to emit streams of eloquent barbs at their opponents' theories. And he kept it up during their weeks of intense legal research and writing.

Moot court is an all-consuming experience, the law school equivalent of a two-week stay at the Betty Ford Clinic. And by the time Nina and Tom were finished with their oral argument, she thought she was in love. She wasn't quite sure what he thought, but the fact that they were both involved with other people did not stop them from quietly slipping out of Boston for a couple of days, once moot court was over. They packed up their cross-country skis and headed north to consummate what had been building over the past month.

By the end of their clandestine weekend, she had found him a little scary. It had started out great, Tom and Nina in a marijuana-infused haze of delayed sexual gratification. But by Sunday morning, he had turned inward. She couldn't draw him out of his deep brood, despite her humorous and sexual attempts. The afternoon's trip had been too quiet for her taste. Back in Boston, they returned to their respective paramours—Nina to her intensely verbal urban ethnic classmate and Tom to the pleasant hometown girl that he would later marry. Nina and Tom hadn't slept together since.

It wasn't the end of it, of course. While still in law school, they periodically had meaningful lunches, where they sometimes discussed whether they wouldn't have made a great couple. And they indulged in a few sessions of wistful kissing. But after graduation, Nina returned to New York and Tom went back to Lake Placid, the town where many Wilsons had practiced law for many generations. The North Country, the land of the deep brooders. He went into practice with his cousin and married Chris. They had a red-haired daughter named Annie. And Tom came into the city occasionally, always making time for a meaningful lunch with Nina.

It wasn't until the last meaningful lunch, about a year ago, that Tom had mentioned the possibility of divorce. It was as if he'd suddenly turned up the heat on a pot that had been simmering just on the verge of a boil. Nina had immediately felt herself drawn back in.

Usually she found herself put off by Tom's eyes, the heavily lidded ones of a marijuana addict. Over lunch they started to look like deep blue pools. His longish, dirtyish hair, which had always struck her as a sign of decay, suddenly gave him the cachet of a French film star. But Nina had pulled herself back. He was an out-of-town married lawyer talking about how his wife didn't understand him. It was all too trite for her to be trapped, she told herself.

But they had parted with a kiss, longer than any they had shared since Boston. And although she hadn't exactly been languishing in Manhattan in a dreamy stupor, obsessing about Tom Wilson, she did think about him from time to time. And today, headed north on the New York State Thruway, she was thinking about him a lot more than she was thinking about Mark Hirsch.

It was dark by the time Nina pulled into Lake Placid, but she had no trouble finding the Whiteface Inn. There it was, right on Lake Placid itself, a few minutes from the center of town. It was a combination of old charm and recent real estate development. She checked in and then called Tom before she unpacked.

"I made it," she said.

"Without too much trouble, I hope."

"It was okay. Although every time I rent a car I think of that scene in *Annie Hall* when Woody Allen flies out to Los Angeles and has to drive. I'm not quite as bad, but it takes me a while to get going."

"Why you live in that unnatural city is beyond me," Tom said. "I think you have the potential to be a normal person."

"We'll never know, will we?"

"What did you think of our town?"

"I hardly got to see it. But from what I did see, it looked pretty. Cold, though."

"It's February and you're in the Adirondacks. What did you expect, sweetheart?" The "sweetheart" did not go unnoticed. But he said it with enough affection and amusement tempering his condescension as to render the word acceptable. "Ready for dinner?" he asked.

"Yes, except that I'm in jeans. Is that all right?"

"Sure." It was a silly question. Probably everyone here wore jeans to dinner. This was out of town.

But when Tom showed up, he wasn't wearing jeans. He had come straight from the office and wore a tweed sport coat over a gray wool vest and brown slacks. He looked more like a professor than a lawyer. Nina supposed it was the look that would instill confidence in clients in a town like this, rather than the nine-hundred-dollar sharpie suit you needed to practice law in New York City.

He looked pretty good to her. Not terribly well-groomed, but pretty good. His hair was long without being stylishly cut and, as usual, could have been cleaner. But it was still in full supply and hadn't faded from the reddish-brown color that made his eyes look very blue. And he seemed a bit paunchier, which could have been a disaster in Armani, but looked fine under the ragg wool vest. It made him seem more huggable.

So she hugged him hello. The hug served to replace a hello kiss, thereby avoiding such difficult questions as cheek or mouth, wet or dry, open or closed.

They both knew enough not to linger in her cabin, which the queen-size bed glaringly dominated. They walked over to the hotel's restaurant. She was hoping for moose antlers and a large stone fireplace and she wasn't disappointed. Nina sensed it wasn't the kind of place you ordered white wine and pasta salad, so she opted for roast chicken and a beer and settled back to see what she might make of Tom Wilson.

"You know," he said, "you really don't look that much different from the way you looked in law school."

It was true in some ways. Considering that her figure had gone when she was about eleven, and that she hadn't been too badly plagued by wrinkles, she really hadn't changed much since puberty. Plumpness was the great antidote for aging. Nina wondered when American women would finally realize this and jump on the bandwagon. Probably not in her lifetime.

"You look pretty much the same too," she said. "Just look at all that hair."

"It's amazing that I haven't pulled it all out," he said.

"I guess it's been a tough year for you, huh?"

"You have no idea. What with my marriage falling apart and my practice breaking up."

"You're not in partnership with your cousin John anymore? How come?"

Tom's gaze went past Nina for a moment. "These are strange times," he said. "Things have really changed in this town. It's not the simple place I grew up in. First there was the Winter Olympics, which resulted in a lot of overbuilding. Then the real estate money started flooding in, chopping everything into time-shares and condos. It changed our practice."

"In what way?"

"I used to spend my days defending drunk drivers and helping people get divorced. People I grew up with."

"And what changed?"

"The nature of the cases. Getting subdivision approvals and filing environmental impact statements and doing the developers' dirty work. Johnny loved it. I shouldn't have been surprised. Even when he was a kid, he was always saving up for an expensive bike and stuff like that."

"And you?"

"Basically, the practice got too fancy for me. And then Johnny started getting paid in ways other than money. You know what I mean?" He didn't wait for an answer. "He got pretty hooked. Between the coke and the expensive suits and the clients making me sick, I finally got fed up. I told him that this wasn't why I had come back to my hometown to practice. I could go to New York City if I wanted this shit."

"He wasn't persuaded?"

"He said he had no interest in changing the direction things were going in. So I busted up the practice. It was right after Chris busted up the marriage. Sometimes I wonder if what I did was a reaction to what she did."

Nina just nodded, adding a small sympathetic grunt.

"So I threw away a lot of business and started over. But I still don't feel the same way about the practice as I did when I first got out of law school. I mean, there are plenty of divorces and drunk drivers. More than ever, it seems. And they still come to me for help. But something inside of me has changed. Each client's divorce or misdemeanor seems like a pool of quicksand that's going to suck me in."

Nina and Tom sat silently for a moment, looking at their beers. "What happened between you and Chris?" she finally got herself to ask.

"It was her decision, really. I can't say I was unhappy being married. I loved my kid and I loved my wife. I still do, if the truth be told. But she kept complaining that I smoked too much dope and that I shut her out. I gave up the stuff for a while. It wasn't easy, believe me. And she still complained that I was in my own world, that I wasn't sharing my life. We went to a marriage counselor, but I still couldn't give her what she wanted. I just didn't know how. It was frustrating. So I stopped going to counseling and started smoking dope again and then she threw me out."

"I'm sorry."

"I haven't got used to it. Every day is constant pain. I only get to see Annie once a week. And when I do see her, I feel guilty for something I don't understand. It's awful. A couple of months ago I moved up to Saranac. I thought it would be easier, not constantly running into my ex-wife and ex-partner. I even opened a second office there. But most of my work is still in Placid, and I'm faced with my ghosts every day."

Tom was that rare person, Nina noted, with whom she had no desire to trade problems.

"How are things going for you?" he asked.

Nina shrugged. "Just one big madcap whirl."

"Life in the big city," he said. "Why do you stay there?"

"Living in New York City is the only thing I'm completely unambivalent about. I have absolutely no desire to leave." It was true. These were times when everyone in New York reassessed, trying to figure out some angle that would get them into a farmhouse in Vermont or onto a houseboat in Sausalito. Nina had no interest. She was, for all intents and purposes, married to New York. Permanently, like a practicing Catholic; pledged at birth, like a Hindu. All separations had been understood to be temporary. "Besides, I'm not so sure that I would play so well out of town."

"I don't know about that. You think we're all too dumb to appreciate you?"

"Maybe I'm being narrow-minded. But I seem to be devoted to New York in a very old-fashioned way."

"Well, I can't say that I find it touching," Tom said. "As far as I'm concerned, the place is a lunatic asylum. And you've voluntarily committed yourself."

"The analogy I've heard is that New York City is a concentration camp, with New Yorkers acting as both the prisoners and the guards. New York–bashing has become a highly developed art form lately."

"How's work?"

"Routine. Housing Court, the Social Security Administration—I find myself speaking the same lines over and over again. Once in a while I come across a case that's a little different. But instead of getting excited, I seem to have that quicksand problem you mentioned."

"Any romantic breakthroughs?"

Nina was suddenly very tired. Too tired to give an animated little tap dance about her amusing yet exasperating love life. About Patrick, last year's heartthrob, who had recently pleaded guilty to voluntary manslaughter. Or Detective James Williams, who had decided to retire and move to California after their second date.

"No romantic breakthroughs," she said.

"How come?"

"It's a bad market. Maybe things will turn around next year. Can we talk about something else?"

"You're the guest."

"Maybe we should discuss our agenda for tomorrow."

"Okay," Tom said. "First I thought we'd go over and talk to the cops. Find out who found the car wreck and how they decided that Hirsch had been drunk when he ran off the road. Then go over to the hospital. Talk to the emergency room staff. Maybe someone has a different opinion from the police."

"Sounds good."

"Maybe the accident report was wrong and he wasn't drunk. Then there's nothing to investigate. We just have a guy who accidentally crashed up his car and that's the end of it. But if what you said is true, that he never drank, and there really was a high level of alcohol in his blood . . . well, that could prove pretty interesting."

"What do I do then?" Nina asked.

"I don't know. Cross that bridge when we come to it."

"Lisa told me that her father left town because he felt threatened. So even if he was murdered, it might have very little to do with Lake Placid. The real investigating might have to be done downstate."

"In a rush to leave already? You just got here." He reached over and took her hand.

Nina looked down at their clasped hands. The guy had some mileage on him. She had already been around with him once, which had culminated in a snowy Sunday afternoon with his silence driving her to tears. And she knew he hadn't changed. His same deep brood had pushed Chris to divorce. And Chris was a woman who had always seemed totally sane. Certainly saner than she felt herself.

But what should Nina expect? She had put some mileage on herself. It was delusional to think that at her age she would come across some sweet, untroubled man who had been sitting around for a couple of decades, just waiting for Nina Fischman.

An old memory came creeping back. She had been a teenager, watching Janis Joplin make an appearance on the *Tonight* show. Janis had just made some reference to her sexual history and Johnny Carson was giving her his studied shocked look. "Oh, did you think I was a virgin?" Joplin asked, her heart tattoo spilling out of her low-cut blouse.

Nina wasn't exactly Janis Joplin, but she wasn't exactly a virgin either. And if she waited around for uncomplicated situations to arise, there would be a lot more waiting than arising going on.

But maybe Tom was beyond complicated. Maybe he was hopeless. The man was still smoking marijuana, for Chrissakes.

Nina lifted her eyes and met his gaze. "I might stick around for a while. We'll see," she said, and put everything off for another day.

10 . . . .

Nina couldn't decide what to wear the next morning—al-
though she usually found getting dressed in the winter a rela-
tively easy proposition. There were all sorts of visual aids
available in the cold weather, like black stockings and pullover sweaters, that you couldn't get away with in the summer.

Nina was basically a cold-weather mammal. With her
thick hair and pale skin and subcutaneous fat, she had a hard
time in the tropics. She was not prepared, however, for the
cold that hit her when she walked over to meet Tom for
breakfast.

She had put on her black pants, as always, along with a
turtleneck and her boiled-wool jacket. The jacket was sort of a
cross between a sweater and a blazer. It came in handy when
you didn't know whether you should be wearing L.L. Bean or
Tahari. Over all that she wore a Thinsulate parka, a vast im-
provement over the down ones that made you look like a
hand grenade. But she was still freezing.

Tom was already there when she arrived at the hotel

restaurant at eight. "I made some calls this morning," he said.

"Already? It's hardly light out." It was one of the reasons Nina would never move out of New York City. All over America, people worked hours like eight to four thirty. At home, lawyers never got in before nine, and it would be considered gauche to arrive home before seven. While out-of-towners ran back to their houses to wash their cars before dinner and shoot a few hoops in the driveway, New Yorkers sat in their offices, waiting for dark. The only ones who left before dusk were the observant Jews rushing home on Fridays for Shabbos.

She ordered granola and two cups of coffee—which might seem incongruous to a hard-core health nut, but Nina didn't really care. Caffeine was the one artificial stimulant she allowed herself on a regular basis, unless you counted *Seinfeld,* the half-hour sitcom on Wednesday nights. She had a huge crush on Jerry Seinfeld. Tom bore some resemblance to him, she thought. There was something about the eyes, the same hyperthyroidy look. She found it appealing on both of them, Tom and Jerry.

"The police chief's down in Albany today," Tom said. "But I've arranged for you to talk to Mel Stoddard, his deputy. Mel's something of a good old boy, but I think he'll help us out."

Mel was a good old boy, all right. Short-cropped gray hair, aviator sunglasses in his shirt pocket, and a military posture. He hardly acknowledged Nina when Tom introduced her. "This is what I meant by my not playing well out of town," she whispered to Tom when Mel stepped down the hall to refill his coffee mug. "I always forget that I'm a member of the second sex until I venture out into America."

"If you don't cut the geocentric crap, I'm going to leave you here alone with Mel," Tom said.

"I'm sorry. But help me out here, okay?"

"Let me do the talking."

"With pleasure," Nina said.

Mel came back with a full coffee cup. He sat down and leaned back in his chair. "Now, what can I do for you folks?" he asked.

"Last December," Tom said, "a man named Mark Hirsch had a fatal car accident right outside of town. Does that ring a bell?"

"I think I remember it. Guy from New York City, right? Driving a rental car." Mel looked at Tom.

Tom looked at Nina. "He might have been driving a rental car," she said. "I'm not really sure." She considered adding that Mark wasn't actually from New York City, but it seemed silly to try to start drawing technical distinctions about living over the Nassau county line. Especially to Mel, who reminded her of Rod Steiger playing a small-town sheriff.

"I'll get the file out." Mel disappeared for a moment and came back with a folder. He sat down at his desk and flipped through some papers. "What do you want to know?" he asked Tom.

"We're trying to establish whether or not Mark Hirsch had been drinking before the accident," he said.

Mel picked up a copy of the accident report. "It says the man was drunk."

Nina got out half a "but" before Tom broke in. "Well, that's mighty surprising to us."

"Why's that?"

"The man didn't drink."

"You know that the man didn't drink?"

"We know that the man didn't drink." They both spoke too slowly for her, but Nina knew enough not to interrupt, that Mel and Tom were performing a carefully choreographed conversational dance. "He couldn't drink," Tom continued. "He was a severe diabetic. Never drank."

"Hmm, maybe we'll get Pete in here. He's the one that found him. Might have something to say." Mel slipped out of the office again.

"Do you know Pete?" Nina asked.

"I know two Petes," Tom said. "We'll see which Pete shows up."

Mel came back in. "Pete's on his way."

"Thanks," Tom said. "We appreciate this."

The deputy sat down again. "Hear you moved up to Saranac."

"I did."

"Not quiet enough around here for you anymore?"

"That's right."

"I know what you mean," Mel said. "Getting so we've got a regular skyline here."

Hardly, Nina thought. She had noticed a few largish buildings in town this morning, but the place wasn't exactly Co-op City.

A young man with light blond hair entered the room. "Pete," said Tom, extending his hand.

"Tom," said Pete, taking it.

"This is Nina Fischman," Tom said. "She's an attorney from New York City. Pete Lyons."

"Ma'am." Pete shook her hand too.

"Ms. Fischman is working on a case involving Mark Hirsch," Tom said.

"The guy who ran himself off the road a couple of months ago?" Pete asked.

"That's right," Mel said. "Your report here says he was drunk. Tom says the guy never drank. What do you remember about it?"

"Oh, he was drunk all right. I'm sure of it. For one thing,

he stank of booze. But I also told the ambulance guys to do a blood check once they got him over to the emergency room. He was already dead, but I thought we should get his alcohol level, for the record. The hospital report should be in the file. Isn't it, Mel?"

Mel fished out another piece of paper. "Jeez," he said. "Hirsch must have poured a fifth of Wild Turkey down his throat right before he took off. He came up with a count of .37."

"What does that mean?" Nina said.

"It means that we could have arrested him just for putting his key in the ignition," Pete said. "Actually, it's amazing that he was still conscious enough to drive. Thirty-seven grams of alcohol per decaliter in your bloodstream is enough to kill some people."

"Did you see the accident?" Nina asked.

"No, ma'am. It was late. I had just finished breaking up a fight in a roadhouse a couple miles outside of town and was thinking about heading back. I saw the car tracks going off the road, so I stopped. Later the medics told me he had been dead for a while, at least an hour."

"What did the accident scene look like?" Nina said.

"Could I take a look at the file for a minute?" Pete asked Mel, who handed it to him.

"No other cars," Pete said, after scanning it. "No ice on the road surface. The road curves around a bit to the left, but not enough for a fence on the side . . . although the shoulder drops off sharply. Between the curve and the drop-off, maybe we should put a fence there. Could go either way. Can't be putting fences everywhere, right?"

"Are you planning on suing us, ma'am?" Mel said. "A wrongful death action for negligent highway maintenance? Something like that?"

Oh great, thought Nina. The combination of her being a

woman, a lawyer, and a New York City Jew was finally kicking in. "No, no. Not at all," she said.

"Ms. Fischman does not represent the Hirsch estate," Tom said calmly. "I would tell you if she did."

"I hope you would," said Mel.

"She's just trying to figure out why Mark Hirsch died with a high alcohol content when he never let any alcohol enter his body."

"Is it the kind of curve that someone could push a car off of?" Nina asked.

"I'd have to take another look," Pete said.

"Could we go out there with you?" Tom asked.

Pete looked at Mel. Mel nodded. "Why don't we all take a ride out there now?" Mel said.

The four of them climbed into a police cruiser and drove a few miles out of town. It was the first time Nina had gotten to see the scenery in the daylight. It was quite something. The Adirondacks didn't have the showy drama of the Rockies or the Alps, but they had a beautiful dignity of their own. They were mountains you could live with.

Snow was piled up on both sides of the highway, but the road surface itself was clear. Pete finally pulled over to the side and turned on his hazard lights. They all got out of the car. "Here's where it happened," he said, pointing. "The car went straight over the side and his head hit the windshield. He wasn't wearing a belt."

It was a perfect place to push someone off the road. The two-lane highway curved gently to the left and downhill. To the right was a steep drop-off. There was no fence. If you put a car in gear and let it go, it would head right off the shoulder and over the edge.

Pete gazed at the drop-off. "I remember the whole thing. He was reeking of booze. I swear he was."

"Maybe we should talk to the hospital staff," Tom said.

"Good idea," Mel said. "Got some time now, Pete?"

"Sure."

"Let's go," Mel said.

My God, thought Nina. If they had been in New York all of them would be frantically feeding quarters into pay phones, trying to get in touch with their offices, seeing if they could clear another forty-five minutes. Instead here they all were, getting everything done right away. Life without appointment books could be remarkably efficient.

The hospital was a few minutes from the center of town. It was small, about the size of a neighborhood elementary school in the city. There was an emergency entrance, but there didn't seem to be a real emergency room. Certainly not one that resembled any that Nina had previously seen. There seemed to be all files and no patients.

There was a cheerful blond woman at the information desk who helped them right away. Of course. She paged a hospital administrator, who arrived immediately. She was no less cheerful, but a little less blond. Mel called her by her first name, which was Betty.

Betty rushed off and pulled Hirsch's file. "Yes," she said, after reviewing the file. "He had a high alcohol content, a blood level of .37. Would you like to speak to someone who was on duty that night?"

"That would be a good idea," said Mel.

She paged a medic named Charles Michaels, who showed up within a few minutes. This guy had dark hair and pimples. Nina was relieved.

"Oh, sure," Michaels said. "No question about it. Hirsch had a lot of alcohol in his system. Too much, if anything. The count seemed too high. I've been doing this kind of work for ten years in the area, and up around here I've seen a lot of inebriated folks. But I'd say that this guy set an all-time record."

"Interesting," said Mel. He turned to Tom and Nina. "Is there anything else we can do for you folks?"

"Not right now," Tom said. "Just a ride back to my car. I'll be in touch."

Mel and Pete dropped them off at Tom's Jeep. "What do you think?" Nina asked him, after Mel and Pete had left.

"Well," he said, "it's clear that the police want you to think that Hirsch was drunk when he went over the side. That way, if you sue them because of the road not being properly fenced, they can hit you with a comparative negligence defense. But it sounds to me like he was drunk."

"It does?" They climbed into Tom's car.

"Yup. But that doesn't mean that someone didn't get him that way and push him off the road. I've been driving these roads for decades. There aren't too many places like that, with no fence and such a steep drop-off. They're careful with the roads. With a combination of icy winters and a high alcoholism problem, they've got to be. Someone knew what they were doing."

"So what happened? They held a gun to his head and forced him to down enough liquor to get him falling-down drunk? And then pushed him off the road, hoping he'd go through the windshield?"

"Maybe."

"There've got to be easier ways to have someone killed," Nina said.

"I think it's pretty clever." Tom turned to her. "Nina, I've got a client coming in soon. Then I have to pick up Annie after school. We usually go to my mother's for dinner on Fridays and then she stays over at my place."

"Oh," she said, trying to sound emotionally neutral.

"I told her that we could go skiing tomorrow before I take her back to her mother. Would you like to come with us?"

"Skiing?" She tried to sound emotionally neutral again.

"Cross-country. No cheap thrills."

"Cross-country." Nina was relieved. She had never gotten over the feeling that downhill skiing was for dumb people. "I'd love to."

"You're staying the weekend, aren't you?"

"I guess so."

"Good. We'll have fun."

She hoped so, but she wouldn't put any money on it. They drove back to her hotel.

"You going to be able to keep yourself occupied until tomorrow?" he asked her.

"Sure. I've got a set of motion papers I'm working on. This will give me a chance to get a jump on them." It was bullshit, she knew. She also had two old issues of *The New Yorker* in her suitcase, which were bound to win out. But the pretense of getting some work done was, among lawyers, like an involuntary tic. And even Nina wasn't immune.

11

The kid had gorgeous hair. The combination of Tom's auburn and Chris's strawberry-blond had produced a shade of bright orange, like the stain that tomato sauce leaves on a white porcelain sink. Annie had fat pigtails and bushy bangs and bright green barrettes in the shape of pickles. She had bright green eyes, too, but there was worry in them. She kept looking apprehensively at Nina throughout the day, trying to figure out who she was and what she was doing there.

Annie and Tom had their own skis, but Nina had to rent a pair. She wasn't as good a skier as the child, but neither of them held a candle to Tom. Nina thought back to their New Hampshire weekend. He had been so graceful, on the slopes and in bed. Masterful. Actually, she didn't remember that much about bed. They had put off sleeping with each other for so long, that Friday and Saturday night had passed in a blurred sexual frenzy.

But the sex must have been pretty damn good, because she remembered waking up Sunday morning and thinking yes, there's nothing like this. It's the most important thing. Nothing else matters as much. Although by the end of Sunday afternoon, after the veil of silence descended, she would have traded all that sex for just a few minutes of decent conversation. By the time they got back to Boston, Nina felt as though she was trapped in a Ingmar Bergman film that wouldn't end.

Tom was great with his daughter. They had matching knickers and gaiters and vests, and Annie followed him around like one of Konrad Lorenz's imprinted baby ducks. It made Nina want to get in line right behind her. Not that she was a sucker for a father figure. As far as men were concerned, she had always gravitated toward the angry, alienated ones. Her youth had been spent in the Yankee Stadium bleachers with a long succession of Red Sox fans.

She managed to stay upright for the first hour or so, but after that she found herself falling a lot. Then her nose began to run and she started to feel a little like a five-year-old. "I'm going back to the lodge," Nina said. "Time for hot chocolate."

"It is getting late," Tom said. "Why don't I drive Annie over to Chris's house while you wait in the lodge?"

"Okay." Nina could understand why he might not want a woman next to him in the Jeep when he pulled up in front of his ex-wife's place.

She could understand, but it made her wonder about Tom and Chris. He had said on Thursday that he still loved his wife, if the truth be told. Those were his exact words. He would probably go back to her if he could. Well, why not? Why not be able to see his daughter for more than one day out of seven? But it made Nina feel beside the point. Like a consolation prize. Maybe she should go back to her hotel room tonight.

That didn't seem to be the plan, however. Tom had said

that he'd cook her dinner, and a seduction seemed in order. She didn't want to fight it, but it was making her nervous. Like waiting for the results of your Pap smear. Probably everything would be okay, but you never knew. To add to her anxiety, she had the out-of-town jitters. She had told Tom that she didn't play well outside of New York, but it was more than that. Out-of-town didn't play so well with her.

There was the ethnic thing, of course. To be suddenly thrust from large groups of short, dark, gesticulating people into a sparsely populated landscape of tall, fair natives who moved only their lips when they spoke—well, it was disconcerting. And the constant apprehension of not knowing whether to make a left or a right at the corner was hard for Nina, who prided herself on her excellent skills as a Manhattan navigatrix. But the real problem was that away from home, she was often struck by the fact that it was, after all, a man's world.

Nina settled into an overstuffed chair in the lodge and looked around. She was surrounded by examples of what could be achieved by male prowess. There were deer heads on the wall, along with bass and pike mounted on walnut plaques. A stuffed beaver stood on a twig table and a bearskin rug covered the floor. A huge blaze roared in the stone fireplace.

Outside, squadrons of snowplows, snowmobiles, and four-wheel-drive vehicles transported men across the frozen landscape. Hunting, fishing, trapping, fire-making, and operating heavy machinery were things that women could learn to do. But only if they were an unusual type of woman and only if they tried extra hard. Of course, there was probably a lot of terrific pie-baking going on in Lake Placid kitchens, despite the lack of marble countertops. But the invisibility of the pie-baking made it seem like it didn't count.

New York City was, in many ways, a woman's town.

There the major activities were, as opposed to moving large piles of snow around, shopping, cab-hailing, theater-going, and negotiating. All things that women were naturally good at. Even the more macho activities, like bond-trading, only required a brain and a mouth, not biceps and deltoids.

Scattered around the lodge were a few couples, with and without children, and a cluster of drinking buddies in plaid flannel shirts and tractor caps. That was another weird thing about being out of town—you never saw women in groups. Back in the city, duos and trios and larger ensembles of women, from twelve years old to ninety, roamed about at all hours without the least bit of self-consciousness. Despite all the nuclear family propaganda the magazines were hurling lately, a woman in New York City could still call her own shots.

Suddenly Housing Court and her cramped apartment seemed appealing. She fought back an urge to bolt, to check out and head south before Tom came back. It would be too easy, Nina told herself, to use neurosis as an excuse for rudeness. But she was still toying with the idea when he appeared. "Ready to go?" he called across the room.

"Ready." She picked up her black leather tote bag and walked over to him. It was the same bag she carried around all week, to the office and the gym. But now it held clean underwear, her wire-bristled hairbrush, and a couple of condoms. That was the great thing about a tote bag. It was a piece of luggage, but not really. It obviated the necessity of committing one way or the other. If you did stay over, you were prepared. But if things didn't work out, you could just pick up what looked like your ordinary purse and go home without any embarrassment.

No wonder there had been so little premarital sex in the days of small handbags. You couldn't very well go out on a date premeditatedly schlepping a suitcase.

During the drive, Tom explained the difference between the towns of Saranac Lake and Lake Placid. And once they got to Saranac, Nina saw what he meant. It didn't feel like a resort, the way Placid did. It had an old-timey feeling, one that came from being worn-out rather than from having been lavishly restored. The town reminded Nina of some old guy who was basically decent, but had known his share of troubles with unemployment and the bottle.

Tom's street was less worn-out than the others, with large respectable houses and tall old trees. His home, with its freshly painted porch and neat white trim, could have housed a doctor and his wife and their five children. "Nice," Nina said as they pulled into the driveway. "Do you own or rent?" It was a question that people in Manhattan asked almost automatically. But Tom gave her a look that made it clear that she had been inappropriate. As if she had just asked for last year's gross income or whether he had gotten laid that week.

"I didn't mean to pry," she added quickly. "I guess I've gotten that real estate disease that people in New York City have."

"And what disease is that?"

"Incessant discussion of real estate prices. It's like an epidemic."

"What would you say accounts for it?" he asked.

"I think it's because the novelty of home ownership still hasn't worn off. All over the rest of the country, you've been buying and selling your houses for decades. Centuries, really. While we always rented."

"And what changed?"

"Here's what I think happened. Somebody came along about fifteen years ago and said, 'Hey, I have a great idea. Let's sell the building to the tenants.' And then everything converted to co-ops and condos and we're all still excited by the idea of appraisals and mortgages and other things you consider old hat. Most New Yorkers are very unsophisticated that way. In the city there are people who are tremendously successful in business and have never even closed on a piece of property."

"I see. And everyone's still obsessed."

"Actually, it's getting better. Since prices started going down, people stopped discussing them. I guess it just got too depressing."

"Well, I'm renting." He sounded like he was asking for sympathy.

"Oh. Well, so am I."

Tom unlocked the door and held it open for her. She walked past him into a large entry hall. It smelled of marijuana. He took her coat and hung it in the hall closet. She followed him into the living room. "Should I make a fire?" he asked. "It seems a little cold."

It was freezing, the way it always was in people's houses. New York City apartments were kept about twenty degrees hotter than most American homes. "Maybe a little cold," she said politely. "A fire would be nice."

Nina sat on the couch while Tom engineered what seemed like spontaneous combustion. He had a successful fire going in about forty-five seconds. It was always sexy watching someone do something well. Whether it was mental or physical, competence was arousing.

The furniture was masculine in an Adirondack kind of way. Green corduroy and tartan plaid wool covered most of it. Tom turned on the radio and Garrison Keillor came on. Perfect for a Saturday night in the North Country. "Want a drink? Or something?" Tom asked, opening a wooden box of perfectly rolled joints.

Nina considered it. It was like time traveling, with National Public Radio playing in the background and the smell of cannabis tempting her. My life isn't like this anymore, Nina thought. Do I miss it? If I hadn't moved back to New York, would I still be living the way I did in law school, carrying a day pack instead of a Coach leather tote, and dancing to the soundtrack of *The Harder They Come*?

But that was a long time ago. People in the city made fun of those hopelessly mired in Birkenstock sandals and reggae music. But who was holier than thou? The Birkenstockers and their detractors seemed to give each other a run for their money.

Nina took a joint and examined it. She had an ambivalent feeling about marijuana. It had been her coming-of-age drug, but she had always found it depressing. But maybe that was because her usage had been confined to her teens and early twenties, the glory years of depression. The years when all parents are convinced that their children are showing signs of a bipolar disorder. Thank God she had made it to her thirties, the age of anxiety. It was so much more fun.

What the hell, she thought. Why waste a perfect setting? She put the joint between her lips and leaned toward Tom for a light.

The first hit brought back a lot of memories. She thought about a brown suede fringed jacket that she had worn to death and wondered what happened to it. She remembered what it had felt like to wear waist-length braids. The cover of an album flashed into her mind, the Grateful Dead's *American Beauty* with a big picture of a rose on it. The lyrics to "Truckin' " ran through her head. It was like a film montage of the counterculture. She took another hit and handed it to Tom.

"It's okay," he said. "Keep it." He lit another for himself. So this was Tom Wilson's version of growing up. Everybody gets their own joint. "Hungry?" he asked.

"For what?" she said boldly.

"You New Yorkers certainly are pushy." He laughed. "Come on, let's eat." He led her into the kitchen.

It was a sight that she didn't get to see in New York very often. A kitchen with a table in it. Her kitchen had a couch in it. Or rather, her living room had her kitchen in it. He pulled a bottle of chardonnay out of the refrigerator and poured two glasses.

"This is the first time I've ever accompanied a joint with wine that didn't come out of a jug," Nina said.

Tom lifted his glass. "To first times," he said.

"To second times," she said, emptied her glass, and kissed him.

12

....

The sex had been good but the food had been better, Nina decided on Sunday morning. She had forgotten that about marijuana, how enthusiastic it made you feel about eating. Not that she generally needed any assistance. And Tom had turned out to be a good cook, in that serious way it sometimes seemed that only men can be.

For women, cooking was mostly something they did on a daily basis, like flossing their teeth. You couldn't take it too seriously or you'd go mad. But for many men, it remained an event, an act of high drama. Recreation instead of work. Recipes were selected with both a seriousness of purpose and great joy. Not like Nina, who chose a recipe simply because she already had most of the ingredients in the house anyway.

Tom was one of those guys. It was odd that these tendencies still remained divided along gender lines, now that so many men and women lived the same lives. Comparing herself with Tom, he should be the one who considered cooking drudgery, with a daughter and attendant domestic responsibilities. Yet he clearly enjoyed it more than she did. The genetic memory must linger on, because Nina refused to follow any recipe that spilled onto a second page.

There was also a little subplot here, she had to admit. To women, food could be dangerous. More dangerous to some than others, of course, but most kept a wary eye. Food wasn't something you could really relax around, while men seemed to be able to enjoy it in a more detached way. When the recipe called for one-half cup of olive oil, they actually used the full amount, instead of automatically reducing it to two tablespoons. Maybe that was why so many things they cooked tasted so good. "Look at this gorgeous veal chop," Tom had boomed enthusiastically the night before, holding it aloft. Nina had taken a quick look, nervously checking it for fat content.

A veal chop wasn't anything she would ever choose to cook, anyway. Roasting slabs of meat late at night was a male preoccupation. A ritual that clearly evolved from the caveman's daily hunt, while his female counterpart had foraged for nuts and berries throughout the day. And noshed. Left to their own devices, most women she knew would still choose to forage. Half a bagel here, a banana there, maybe some frozen yogurt in a little while. Sitting down to a slab of roasted meat at night was something they did only for some man.

Not that Tom's veal chops weren't delicious. He had coated them with a mixture of bread crumbs and Parmesan cheese and sautéed them in olive oil. And he had made the salad dressing with freshly squeezed lemon juice. For dessert, there was crème brûlée, artfully branded with a hand salamander he had ordered from the Williams Sonoma catalog. He had done everything right.

And he had been just as skillful getting her into bed. Though it hadn't been hard. By that time Nina had given herself over, the way tourists do abroad. *I don't speak the language, I don't know the roads, what the hell, I'll follow this guy's lead.* Besides, watching Tom masterfully press the red-hot sizzling salamander into the quivering flesh of the crème brûlée custard had been a turn-on. And now, sitting at the kitchen table the next morning, drinking coffee and eating a homemade jalapeño muffin, Nina cautiously waited to see if Tom was going to go into Sunday withdrawal, like last time.

He was already primed for it, with his head in the Sunday paper. But wait a minute, here he was, putting the paper down and lifting his head. And actually speaking to her. "We might get some more snow today," he said.

"In that case, I better hit the road pretty soon." There, that should help. In Nina's experience there was nothing like a time limit to make a couple relax. Which was probably why things had gone so well last night. They both knew that she was getting the hell out of there the next day.

It seemed to work. "I'm going to miss you," he said. "It was really great having you here."

"I had a wonderful time too." My God, here they were, like two grown-up characters in a Noël Coward play, being polite and mutually appreciative. Maybe there was hope for this generation after all.

A slightly awkward pause ensued. Uh-oh, Nina thought. Timing was everything. If she let the pace lag, it could be fatal. With an instinct for survival she didn't know she had, she suddenly remembered something about men. They liked to discuss topics. Real topics, not existential ones like relationships and mothers. "Do you think the police are covering something up?" she asked, mostly to prevent the conversational ball from flying into foul territory.

"What do you mean?" he said, apparently with real interest.

Now she actually had to pursue this topic. "You said that

it was important to the police that they convince me that Mark was drunk, so they would have a comparative negligence defense in case Mark's estate sued because of negligent highway maintenance. But maybe it's more than that. Maybe they don't want word of a suspicious death leaking out. After all, it is tourist season. The last thing they need is a murder."

It was the first time the thought had even occurred to Nina. In a scramble to keep Tom engaged in conversation, she had come up with this theory off the top of her head. But once it was out, it sounded plausible to her. Well, she had always worked well under pressure.

"I wouldn't say that they were covering anything up," Tom answered. "But then again, I wouldn't say that they went out of their way to figure out what happened. They were doing their job, but that's about it. That's about all you can expect these days."

"I guess you should consider yourself lucky if you get people to do their job."

"I do think the hospital messed up, however."

"In what way?" asked Nina.

"They said that Hirsch showed a lot of alcohol in his blood. They should have been suspicious."

"You're not going to give me any of that 'Jews don't drink' crap, are you?" Nina said. "Because it's not true. Maybe it used to be, but this generation is different. More assimilated. Probably from having gone away to college. Boozing is right up there with playing tennis and marrying Christians."

"That's not what I meant. Although if you stuck around and spent a winter in the Adirondacks, you might have a better idea of what real boozing is."

She decided not to dwell on whether or not this counted as a suggestion that she stick around. Stay on the topic, she cautioned herself. "What do you mean by the hospital messing up?"

"Well, you said he was a severe diabetic. That means he was injecting insulin, right?"

"Probably."

"Which would mean needle marks. Someone should have noticed," Tom said, "and figured out he was a diabetic. Which would have made them suspicious about the alcohol. But again, I guess they were just doing their job, nothing more."

"I suppose I have a few things to look into when I get back to New York. I'll have to confront Beverly all over again. And try to see what else Lisa knows. Not to mention having to probate Helen Hirsch's estate. That should be fun."

"Probating an estate like that is good practice."

"For what?" No matter how hard she tried, Nina couldn't help feeling that anything that made you a better lawyer was wasted on her.

Breakfast continued to go well. Nina managed to stay on the topic and Tom managed to stay somewhat engaged. Although she did notice that he pulled out a joint with his second cup of coffee and smoked it, even though she declined his offer to share. This was not good, smoking alone before noon.

None of them were perfect, she told herself as she headed downstate on the Northway. He could be worse. It could have been crack he was smoking, instead of grass. Or he could have tendencies toward violence instead of silence. Then she remembered that these were the kinds of excuses that kept women in all sorts of abusive relationships. It was something you read about in all the magazines. If you found yourself saying "He could be worse," it was supposed to be a red flag. And a red flag was not a promising start to a relationship.

But was this a relationship they were starting? It remained unclear. Their farewell had been light and cheerful and noncommittal. He had told her he couldn't wait to see her again, but he had made the sentiment sound mild, not going out of his way to sound convincing.

She supposed it was possible that she might never even see him again. That thought cheered her up a bit. My God, she was getting as bad as he was. Is this what happens to women who don't bear children before the age of thirty-five? Their estrogen level drops and their fear of intimacy rises? Next she'd be growing a beard and developing a pleasant baritone. Well, maybe smaller hips would be a side benefit.

As Yonkers became the Bronx, Nina made a decision to keep the rental car for another week. Garaging it would cost a fortune, but it would make her life so much easier. She'd need to go out to Helen's apartment again, and pay another visit to Beverly. She could live without the Long Island Rail Road.

Besides, she was enjoying driving around. She liked the way the car handled, even if it was only a Chevy Corsica. Just having her hands on the wheel made her feel powerful. Maybe she *was* turning into a man. She rubbed her palm against her cheek, checking for stubble, as she sped through Riverdale.

13

Something strange happened in the Bronx, as it had so many times in her life. Nina found herself heading toward the Whitestone Bridge. She was exhausted and knew she should have headed straight home, but she couldn't stop. She wanted to talk to Beverly. Right now, while she remained in drive. Before she had to put the car in the neighborhood garage and become a powerless pedestrian again.

She had a vague idea that the Clearview would take her to the Long Island Expressway, and her hunch paid off. The Great Neck exit on the highway was easy to find. From there she tried to follow the path that the cute Israeli cabdriver had taken.

Nina had to circle around Manhasset Hills a couple of times, but she finally hit on Executive Drive. The red Toyota Celica and the gray Mercedes were both in the driveway. She thought about turning back. It would be tricky to question Beverly with Stuart Grossman there. On the other hand, maybe something interesting would develop.

She parked behind Grossman's car and rang the bell. The dog barked right away, but it took a while for someone to come to the door. Nina checked her watch. It was ten-thirty at night, an absurd time to be ringing someone's bell without warning. Finally Beverly showed up, in an oversize T-shirt and pink brocade high-heeled mules. She stared at Nina through the screen door without saying anything.

"Hello?" Nina finally said, more of a question than a greeting.

"I guess you want to come in." Beverly sounded pissed. And maybe a little scared.

"If I may."

Beverly opened the door and let Nina into the house. "Who is it?" Stuart Grossman called from the top of the stairs. When Beverly didn't answer, he came downstairs to see for himself. He wore gray sweatpants and no shirt. He looked at Nina and then at Beverly for an explanation.

"That person who's the executor of Helen's estate," Beverly said, then shrugged.

"Nina Fischman," Nina said, extending her hand.

"Stuart Grossman," he said, shaking it. He was fuzzy all over, like a gray rabbit. Gray hair covered his barrel chest, his shoulders, his arms, and his sizable gut. Nina resisted an urge to pet him. The hair on his head was also gray. None of it seemed to be missing. It was wavy and combed straight back, like a bandleader in the forties. His eyebrows were thick and black and underneath his eyes a pair of black bags mirrored the brows. His eyes were dark and controlled as they examined Nina.

Beverly's eyes darted anxiously from Stuart to Nina. The three of them waited to see what would happen next. Finally Stuart spoke. "What can we do for you?"

"I wanted to ask Beverly a few questions."

"About what?" he said.

"About what I discussed with her last week."

"Don't you think it's kind of late?" Beverly said. "We're tired."

"So am I." Nina decided to get pushy. "I wouldn't mind some coffee, actually."

"Oh, you wouldn't, would you?" Stuart had a Brooklyn accent, the male counterpart of Beverly's. Maybe even heavier.

Nina found herself smiling at him. He might have meant it in a threatening way, but she was always attracted to sarcasm in men. It came from growing up with a Jewish father. She looked Grossman over again. There was a crudeness about him. All that body hair covering the thick torso, the bags under the eyes, and the New York street accent. But he was not unattractive, if you were into that type.

The dog ran downstairs and sniffed Nina's toes. "Lisa," Beverly called, "get Bunny out of here. Right now. And then go back to bed."

Lisa emerged from the spot at the top of the stairs recently vacated by Grossman and came down to retrieve the dog. She wore a flannel nightgown with little pastel sheep all over it. "Hi," she said to Nina, and picked up Bunny.

"Hi, Lisa. Hi, Bunny." Nina let the dog lick her hand. Lisa and Bunny made a cute couple. Maybe it wouldn't have been so bad to have had a dog as your younger sibling, Nina thought. It was a less competitive situation. If the dog had puppies, you could play with them without feeling like an old maiden aunt.

"I'll make coffee," Beverly said wearily. "Decaf?"

"I think I could use some caffeine," Nina said.

"Fine." She turned to Stuart. "Maybe you should put on a shirt."

"Okay," he said, slapping his gut. It was amazing how some old guy could parade around, showing off a piece of anatomy that a woman would spend entire therapy sessions obsessing about.

While Beverly was in the kitchen making coffee and Stuart was upstairs getting dressed, Nina wandered around the living room, examining the contents of the wall unit. My mother would disapprove, she thought. Ida was very judgmental about such things. She spurned the kind of *chotchkas* that Beverly collected, favoring primitive ethnic artifacts. Everything had to be carved wood or unglazed clay. She would never allow any of Beverly's Lladró porcelain figures into her house. It was as if displaying anything from Africa, Asia, or South America automatically made you a person of higher morals and deeper intellect.

Lladró porcelain was bad enough, but not nearly as reprehensible as Hümmel figures. Ida had raised Nina to fear and loathe those gaily colored ceramic kinder frolicking in the wald. To her mother, they represented all that was wrong in the world.

This was a controversy that had apparently raged among many older Jewish women. For Ida was not the only one whom Nina had heard contemptuously dismissing another woman as a collector of Hümmel figures. The controversy seemed to have ended with Nina's generation, which favored minimalism. An important piece of glass and maybe an oversize amethyst geode, that was about it. Never a cherubic porcelain fräulein weaving an edelweiss chain. So the Idas of the world had prevailed after all.

Stuart came downstairs wearing a sweatshirt that matched his gray sweatpants. He had also added what looked like a gold Rolex watch.

"Coffee's ready," Beverly called. "Why don't you both come into the kitchen?" Nina followed Beverly's voice and found herself in a room lined with black lacquer cabinets. The place did not exactly exude homey warmth. It was the kind of room that forced you to take out the Glass Plus every ten minutes.

Nina and Stuart sat down at the kitchen table, while Beverly poured coffee into two mugs. Both mugs had pictures of dinosaurs on them. One dinosaur was laden with parcels and was, according to the mug, a shoposaurus. The other dinosaur, who was exercising, was an aerobosaurus. Nina couldn't help thinking to herself what a real schmuckosaurus Beverly was.

Nina prayed that there was something more potent than skim milk in the refrigerator. Two percent was Nina's minimum requirement for coffee. Anything thinner turned it gray. She didn't hold out much hope, however. The woman looked like she mainlined skim milk.

But Nina lucked out. Stuart asked for half-and-half and got it. Nina cut in on his action and gave herself a healthy hit. She happily watched the tiny globules of fat float on the surface of her coffee. What the hell, she thought. These days, dairy products were a controlled substance in her life. A couple of fat globules once in a while weren't going to condemn her to death.

In the center of the table sat a Lucite container filled with blue packets of Equal and pink packets of Sweet'n Low. Stuart went for the blue. Nina scorned both, ignoring her usual impulse to do as the natives do. That didn't hold true out here in NutraSweet country.

The coffee tasted a little strange. "Interesting," Nina said.

"I used chocolate-amaretto beans," Beverly told her with pride.

A real schmuckosaurus. At least the beans weren't artificially sweetened, thought Nina as she forged ahead with her coffee. "Aren't you having any?" she asked Beverly.

"Just water," she said, and poured herself a glass. Nina

hated women who always ordered "just water" as much as her mother hated women who always wore high heels. Well, that wasn't technically true, because Nina often stuck with water through a meal. But some women spoke the words "just water" with sickening self-righteousness. Beverly was one of them.

"What is it that you wanted to discuss?" Stuart asked.

"I've just spent a very interesting weekend in Lake Placid." Beverly flinched at "Lake Placid." It reminded Nina of the old vaudeville routine, the one where the comedian goes nuts every time someone says "Niagara Falls."

"What were you doing there?" Stuart said calmly.

Nina went on to relate most of what had transpired upstate, leaving off before Tom and the veal chops. Beverly made like she had something to say a few times, but Stuart silenced her with a gesture that indicated that she might want to consider keeping her mouth shut.

"What do you want from Beverly?" he asked.

"I can't reveal my sources," Nina said, "but it has come to my attention that Beverly hired a private detective right after Mark disappeared. Apparently the detective located Mark in Lake Placid and informed Beverly of his whereabouts. Since it appears that Mark was murdered, the fact that Beverly knew where he was starts to look a little weird."

"Miss Fischman," Stuart said, "I pay taxes. Not as much as the government may like, perhaps, but what I consider to be a substantial sum. And part of what the government does with my tax money is hire competent law enforcement professionals to make sure that crimes do not go unpunished. This does away with the need for nosy little amateurs like yourself to poke their *shnozzolas* into places where they do not belong. Do you get my drift?"

It was all too easy for a guy with black bags under his eyes and a gold Rolex on his wrist to make Nina feel like a small dried-up dog turd. She fought the feeling, but felt herself going under. She turned her gaze away from Stuart and looked at Beverly, who was breathing in sharp little whimpering gasps. "Tell me the name of the private detective that you hired."

"Kevin Karp," Beverly answered without a pause.

Nina didn't know whether or not to believe her. It seemed such an unlikely name for a detective. Nina, having very little experience with private detectives, expected an Italian or Irish name. Not Karp. Karp was her uncle Harry's name, not the name of someone who carried a gun. And Kevin just didn't go with Karp. There were Jewish Kevins, but most of them were no more than sixteen years old. Beverly could easily be lying.

But Nina decided now was not the time to find out. Not with the Gross Man (as Lisa had referred to him) sitting at the table, guarding Beverly. Nina could always come back if there turned out to be no Kevin Karp. Preferably at a time when Stuart wasn't there.

"Thank you," Nina said to Beverly, and walked out the door without glancing in Stuart's direction.

14 . . . .

Kevin Karp was 100 percent Irish. Nina was sure of it. He had a small upturned nose and a big brown walrus mustache. And he was at least forty-five, way too old to be a Jewish Kevin.

"Interesting name," she said, after he had shown her into his office. "Unusual ethnic mix."

"My mother's second husband was Jewish," Karp explained. "He adopted me and I took his last name. Mom was thrilled. It was her idea of upward mobility."

"I see. I hope you didn't mind my prying."

"Oh, no," he said. "I get a lot of questions about it. I don't exactly look like a Karp."

That was putting it mildly. Karp stood out on him like a sore thumb. It was a well-known phenomenon, but unusual on a man. There were plenty of small-nosed Virginias and Christinas in New York dangling Epstein and Shapiro surnames as if from a charm bracelet. But on a man it seemed odd. Yet another manifestation of societal sexism.

Kevin Karp had been easy to find. One call to Nassau County directory assistance had been all it took. He had been extremely cooperative, making himself available on Monday after Nina got off work. And giving her explicit directions, so she didn't get lost once in the rental car.

Kevin Karp's office was in Mineola, near the courthouse. It was on the top floor of a two-story taxpayer, over a travel agency. He shared a suite of offices with a podiatrist and an optometrist. The waiting area featured orange molded plastic chairs and synthetic avocado shag carpeting. Beverly would have found the place tacky. Nina wondered who could have recommended Karp to her.

His office looked a little better than the waiting room, with a nice old-fashioned but beat-up oak desk and a brass banker's lamp with a green glass shade. It had the feeling of a second-rate men's club.

"Thank you for seeing me so soon," Nina said. "I must say, I was surprised at how accommodating you were."

"Well, I was expecting your call," he said. "I'm not necessarily that nice first thing in the morning. Or even later in the day."

"Why were you expecting my call?"

"Beverly Hirsch got to me before you did."

"Are you going to have a problem discussing this case with me?" she asked.

"I always have to be careful about confidentiality. But Mrs. Hirsch told me to cooperate with you fully. To tell you whatever seemed relevant."

"She did?" That didn't quite jibe with Grossman's warning about keeping her *shnozzola* out of other people's business.

"Are you surprised?"

"Frankly, I am."

"Why? Did you think she was hiding something?"

"Well, yes," Nina said. "She hasn't been very forthcoming with me. And her boyfriend told me to mind my own business. He was rather abrupt, in a way that I've only seen portrayed in movies directed by Francis Ford Coppola."

"So she has a boyfriend, does she? That was fast. Although I'm not surprised."

"Yeah, she doesn't seem to be of a very independent spirit."

"It wasn't her spirit that I was thinking of," Karp said, playing with his mustache and making his eyebrows go up and down.

"I guess she's okay, if you like tall, thin, long-legged types. I keep waiting for the look to go out of style, but it never does." She had been to the Metropolitan Museum recently and saw a Toulouse-Lautrec nude of a prostitute in a bordello. It was painted from the rear and the model had short legs and a full bottom. It would have been swell, Nina thought, to have lived in an age when hookers had short legs. These days, the Eleventh Avenue whores had legs so long you could swear they were men. Actually, many of them were. Which didn't make Nina feel particularly terrific either.

"Anyway," Karp said, "what is it exactly that you would like to talk about?"

"Did you know that her husband was killed in a car accident?"

"Yeah, she told me a few days after it happened."

"Did she tell you that it was a suspicious car accident?"

"No, just that he was dead."

Nina decided not to go into details just yet. "I'm interested in a couple of things," she said. "Like dates. When did she hire you to find her husband, and when did you find him? And what happened once you found him? Did you make contact with him? When did you find out that he was dead? And, finally, do you have any ideas about how he got that way?"

The file was already on his desk. He opened it. "On Friday, November thirtieth, I got a call from Beverly Hirsch. She came in to see me that afternoon and told me that her husband had disappeared earlier that week. She had no idea where he was. I interviewed his child, his mother, and his business partners. They had various theories as to why he had disappeared, but no one knew where to find him. Then on Monday, December tenth, I got a call from Beverly. She told me that her mother-in-law, Helen Hirsch, had heard from him that morning."

"Can you beat that?" Nina said. "He called his mommy." So much for Las Vegas and long-legged wives and poker games. Mark was, after all, a good Jewish son. "Did he tell Helen where he was?"

"Not exactly. I called Helen Hirsch right away, of course. She told me that her son had phoned just to tell her that he was okay. Not much more, except that he did mention that he was upstate and that he had a new job selling real estate. He hoped he'd be able to come back soon, but that he couldn't just yet. And that to tell Lisa he was sorry he wasn't able to communicate with her, but that he missed her."

So Mark was willing to place a call to his mother's house, but not to his own. And he sent a message to his daughter, but not to his wife. Very interesting. "How'd you find him? New York is a big state."

"There aren't too many towns upstate where you could find a job selling real estate in the winter. In most places it's not exactly prime season. So I figured he had to be selling near a ski resort. Probably condos or time-shares. That's what most skiers seem to be buying."

"Very good." Nina was impressed.

"After all, it's what I do for a living."

"So how did you narrow it down to Lake Placid?"

"I got out the Sunday *Times* real estate section and looked for likely ads. I called the ones near ski areas that specified that they were a broker's listing. It's state law that brokers have to disclose that in every ad they place. I made a lot of calls to Hunter and Windham and Placid, asking for Mark Hirsch. Finally, on one of the Lake Placid ones, I got a 'sorry, he's not in right now.' So I headed right up there and staked out the brokerage."

"Did he show up?"

"Right away. I sat in a car across the street. Too damn cold to stand outside."

"I can imagine."

"Mrs. Hirsch had given me a picture of him. I first spotted him coming out, so I tailed him to his motel on the outskirts of town."

"When was this?"

Karp looked at his file. "Friday, December fourteenth."

"Then what happened?"

"I called Beverly Hirsch from Lake Placid and told her where he was staying. She told me to stay put until she gave me further instructions. She called back a few hours later and told me to go home."

"So what did you do?"

"I got into my car and drove home. I mean, I don't hang around in subzero weather unless I'm getting paid to."

What if some pothead who was once great in bed is feeding you veal chops and crème brûlée, Nina thought. Then would you? "Do you think he knew he was being followed?" she asked.

"No way." Here it comes, she thought. The part where he tells me what a great detective he is. But she was wrong. "We were in the middle of a goddamn blizzard. I doubt whether he took his eyes off the road for even a split second."

"When was the last time you heard from Beverly Hirsch?"

"Well, I called her on Monday the seventeenth, after I got back. Mostly we discussed finances. She told me that she would have no further need of my services and that I should go ahead and send her a bill. So I did. And she sent me a check the next week." He glanced at his file. "I got it on Wednesday, December twenty-sixth, with a note that explained about the car accident. And thanked me for my services and instructed me to close the case."

"And that was it?"

"That was it."

"So you haven't heard the latest. What do you make of this? According to the cops, Hirsch drove himself off the road in a drunken stupor. Very convenient for everyone, right? Especially Beverly, who has both the insurance proceeds and her rich new boyfriend securely in place. Except for one thing. Mark Hirsch never drank. He was a severe diabetic who never touched the stuff."

Karp's face registered several emotions in a row. First his mouth opened in surprise. Then his eyes narrowed into calculating slits. Then a mask dropped over his face, guarding against any further interpretation on Nina's part. "It's strange." He paused. "But I couldn't really hazard a guess as to what happened."

"Would you be available if I were able to arrange for the retention of your services in connection with this case?" Nina might be able to justify paying Karp to solve Mark's murder. It could come out of Helen's estate. After all, Lisa was the beneficiary and she had instructed Nina to find out what happened. Although this was the kind of thing that could get her into trouble—breach of fiduciary duty due to extreme yenta tendencies.

"I don't think that would be possible."

HEADING UPTOWN

"Why not?"

"I'm unavailable at this time," he said with finality. "Now, anything else I can help you with?" He looked at his watch as a broad hint.

That was a quick switch. All of a sudden he had clammed up when she mentioned the possibility of murder. Wasn't murder just the kind of thing that was supposed to get a guy like Kevin Karp really going? Something was screwy here. "No, I guess that's it." Nina got up to leave. "Thank you, you've been very helpful."

"My pleasure."

She opened the door and caught sight of the plastic chairs and shag carpeting. It reminded her of something. She turned around to face Karp. "By the way," she said. "How did Beverly come to hire you? Had you ever worked for her before?"

"No," he said.

"Then how did she find you?"

He hesitated. "I had done some work for one of her late husband's business associates."

"I see." Nina stepped out into the waiting area. As she turned to close the door behind, she saw that Karp was already dialing his phone.

15 . . . .

Nina was too restless to go home. She had dropped the car off at the garage, but somehow she was still in drive. On nights like this, she used to meet her old friend Susan Gold at La Fortuna, a coffeehouse on Seventy-first near Columbus. But she avoided the place these days. For one thing, it reminded her of Susan, whom Nina missed terribly since her death last year. But more to the point, the last plate of biscotti she had consumed there had been shared with a man who had turned out to be far more sociopathic than her usual Upper West Side dating attempts.

She stopped at a phone booth and rang her mother. Ida was in and receiving guests. No, there was nothing in the house to eat except cottage cheese. Nina considered cottage cheese to be the food of oppression. Nothing else had such connotations of slavery and deprivation. Besides, it was disgusting stuff. Joan Rivers was right, it did look like something that somebody else had already eaten.

Nina picked up a quart of wonton soup on her way over.

It was acceptable to eat wonton soup again. Her generation had spent so many years scorning it, consuming vast quantities of hot and sour soup to prove that they had left their parents in the cultural and culinary dust. Now that this prolonged period of gastronomic adolescence was over, many people had given up this edible equivalent of hard rock music and gone back to wonton soup. Thank God. Not that hot and sour soup wasn't all right in certain circumstances. But it was never meant to take the place of wonton soup.

Ida lived in a more desirable apartment building than her daughter did. Nina lived in a walk-up on a side street in an apartment house that didn't qualify as a brownstone. It was what the building inspectors referred to as an old-law tenement. Meanwhile, Ida had doormen and elevators and a laundry room and a compactor chute. All of which were great luxuries in Manhattan.

It was a source of some humiliation to Nina, who had spent years telling condescendingly amusing anecdotes about her humble Bronx parents to the overprivileged New Englanders with whom she had attended law school. Then suddenly, through the vagaries of Uncle Irving and a quirky New York real estate market, Ida had found herself the owner of a two-bedroom prewar apartment in a building on West End Avenue that would, in a better market, sell for half a million dollars. Even in this soft market, it would still sell for more than Nina expected to earn from now until the end of the century. The fact that on Shabbos Ida's neighbors could walk to Zabar's, the current temple of preference among New York's elite Jews, upped its value another hundred grand.

Ida's decor was eclectic, to be kind. Eccentric, to be less kind. Somewhat tacky, to be accurate. It wasn't that the woman didn't have flashes of sheer decorating genius. Her gray flannel deco sofa was spare and elegant. It could have stood in the 1937 living room of a successful film director with leftist leanings. And the blond Herman Miller bedroom bureau and the original Eames chair all stood as a testament to the fact that the apartment belonged to someone who at one time knew what they were doing.

But overlaid upon the still-elegant basics was a thick residue of accumulated junk. Some of it wasn't junk, actually. There were some fine specimens of pre-Columbian pottery, and thoughtful, provocative black-and-white photos on the wall. There was a knockout of a rug, personally schlepped back from Turkey, and an impressive collection of kilim pillows. But there was also a lamp made of glued-together clam shells and a señorita with a big ruffled skirt that covered Ida's spare roll of toilet paper. These were items that her mother had inherited directly, through the exchange of gifts. Or indirectly, from the compactor room, a favorite spot.

It wasn't as if Ida was one of those crazy old ladies who went through the garbage in the street. But if perchance, while throwing her bagged remains down the chute, she happened to spot a perfectly fine set of plastic salt and pepper shakers shaped like snowmen—well, maybe they weren't exactly a design statement, but it was a *shondah*, a shame, to let them go to waste. It was the curse of the immigrant's daughter. Nina thanked God that her ancestors had the foresight to flee Poland during the last century, leaving her grandmother and mother to do the dirty work.

Not that Nina was that much better than Ida. She was, in her own way, a compulsive recycler. She had to force herself to throw out cheese rinds and yogurt containers that no longer had even the merest shred of edible material clinging to them. And if you looked into her closet, you'd find most of her law school wardrobe, stuffed into garbage bags, waiting to be cut up and used as dusting rags. Considering that Nina only saw fit to dust once every leap year, the supply would last her through the next two millennia.

She wasn't as bad as her mother, but neither of them was as good as Laura, Nina's younger sister, who lived a rarefied existence in a Park Slope brownstone and a Westhampton cedar-shingled beach house. Laura kept a fine filter around her houses, letting in only pedigreed items of Victorian and Shaker design.

Nina plopped onto the gray flannel couch, slid a kilim pillow behind her back, pushed the imitation Steuben glass to one side of the coffee table and opened her wonton soup. She had always loved wontons. There was something about food wrapped up in other food that gave off an extra air of mystery and intrigue. Kreplach, pirogi, Jamaican beef patties, spanikopita, they all gave her a kick. Even beef Wellington, with all its Waspy pretensions, held allure.

"They don't give you those noodles anymore," Ida observed sadly, as if she were mourning the passing of a major perk of Western civilization.

"Those noodles were stupid," Nina said. "They tasted like hell, unless you dipped them in duck sauce. Now, there's something I miss—duck sauce."

"They still give you duck sauce when you take out. Along with soy sauce in those little plastic packets."

"They give it to you, but you're not supposed to eat it. Duck sauce is no longer culinarily acceptable."

"I see. Well, I liked those stupid noodles. And I wasn't the only one. I remember when I used to go to Weight Watchers meetings on Pelham Parkway and everyone always asked the lecturer all these questions about how much Chinese food they were allowed to eat on program. And she never knew right off the bat, but had to go consult the management during the week and come back to us with an answer. And she had always told us that those noodles were strictly prohibited. And then one week the word came down from above. One ounce of noodles were now officially the equivalent of one bread and two fats."

"And there was rejoicing in the street," Nina said. "The White Plains Road el was festooned with flowers and people danced the hora all the way up to Allerton Avenue."

"Not quite, but we were pleased. And then there was much discussion about how to estimate an ounce of noodles without bringing your scale to Wong's Palace."

"Mother, I know that in some ways I have it rougher than you did. The economy is shrinking and the men I might once have considered marrying are all busy pursuing early-admission candidates to Bryn Mawr. But I wouldn't change places with you for all the tea in China. Or all the noodles."

"Do you think they actually have those kinds of noodles in China? Aren't they an American invention, like sweet wine at Passover?" Ida didn't wait for an answer. "Anyway, what have you been up to?"

Nina filled her in, again leaving out Tom and the veal chops, but adding a description of her visits to Beverly Hirsch and Kevin Karp.

"Funny," Ida said when Nina had finished. "I wouldn't have thought that she collected Lladró. The marble eggs make sense. I could even see a collection of those stupid little crystal animals that sit on their own mirrors. But Lladró seems a little old ladyish and sentimental for her. Too whole-some for the likes of Beverly Hirsch."

"So I take it you don't think of Beverly as the wholesome type?" Nina asked.

"Not quite."

"Do you think of her as unwholesome enough to have her husband killed?"

"You know the answer to that."

Nina crossed the room and looked at the latest photos of Laura's children on the wall unit. There, next to a picture of

Danielle in a floppy sun hat, was a small crystal mouse. Nina delicately picked it up to examine.

"Wait a minute, Ma. Let me ask you one question. Isn't this one of those little crystal animals that a mere thirty seconds ago you described as stupid?"

"Well, yes, but I didn't pay money for it. And I certainly don't collect them. I have only one specimen."

"How did you happen to come by this item?"

"A neighbor's daughter gave it to me when she was cleaning out the apartment after her mother died."

"Mrs. Gross?"

"No, someone on the eleventh floor."

"God, Ma, now you're working the eleventh floor?"

"I'm not *working* the eleventh floor. I just happened to have developed a relationship with a very nice elderly woman who unfortunately—"

"Okay, okay. Forget it. Let's get back to the topic. Do you really think Beverly Hirsch had her husband killed?"

"Well, it doesn't look good, does it?" Ida said. "First of all, they obviously had a difficult marriage. And according to Helen, Mark had been having a lot of business problems lately. Beverly admitted to you that he had a life insurance policy of which she was the beneficiary. Right?"

"Right."

"Then Mark disappears, maybe hiding from creditors. Beverly hires a private detective who finds him and six days later he's dead. The next time she's seen, it's with a rich boyfriend in her bed. What do you think?"

"I certainly haven't ruled her out. But I'm worried that I'm prejudiced against her. That I'm just looking to find her guilty because of who she is," Nina said.

"That's ridiculous. The facts are the facts. The real reason that you're reluctant to consider her guilt is that it's trite."

"What do you mean?"

"The sexy widow with the smoking gun is just too pre-dictable for you. You want something quirkier, more surpris-ing. Generally, the truth is that the person you think did it, did do it."

"Maybe you're right," Nina said. "Or maybe I don't want Beverly to be guilty, for Lisa's sake. What if she was guilty? What would happen to the child? And don't tell me that she'd be better off."

"Lisa certainly wouldn't be better off. The question is whether or not she'd be worse off."

"I guess she's doomed to a life of psychotherapy, no mat-ter what happens. When I took her out for ice cream, she made herself throw up."

"Poor thing."

Nina took her empty wonton soup container into the kitchen and tossed it into the trash. When she came back into the living room, she lay down on the sofa. "What do I do next?" she asked.

"Do you think you could find out anything more from that private detective? Maybe he's hiding something. Or at least being evasive."

"I don't think I'm going to get anything else out of him."

"Too bad."

"There is one thing I didn't mention. He acted pretty strange when I asked who referred Beverly to him. Which I would think would be a pretty innocent question. He hesi-tated, looking nervous, and then said something about one of Mark's business associates. It makes me wonder."

"You should be interviewing Mark's partners. Helen al-ways said they were a pretty grotesque pair."

"I wouldn't even know how to find them."

"Call Mark's office number and see what happens."

Nina got up to get her purse. "I've been carrying around Helen's phone book, since there are about a dozen calls I've been meaning to make in connection with her estate. I have to arrange to pay all her debts. There are bills from doctors and Con Edison and Visa and MasterCard."

"She wasn't running a balance on her credit cards, was she?"

"I don't know. Why?"

"Old Jewish ladies never do. They'd rather die than pay seventeen percent."

"Know thyself." Nina rummaged through her pocketbook. She pulled out a very beat-up phone book, the one with the blue Mary Cassatt print on the cover that they sell at the Metropolitan Museum of Art. "Mark's office number should be in here." She turned to the H's. "Here it is, Mark at work. I'll call tomorrow."

"Why don't you try now?"

"Because it's almost ten o'clock at night."

"Aren't you curious?"

Nina rose to the challenge. No one was going to accuse her of not being curious. She dialed Mark's number. "You have reached 555-2990. The number has been changed. The new number is"—the recorded voice paused, trying to convey a sense of excitement and expectancy—"area code 516-555-3921." Nina repeated the number under her breath until she got to a pad and pencil. "There's a forwarding number," Nina said. "What should I do?"

"Call it."

Nina dialed the number. She put her hand over the mouthpiece. "My God," she said. "Somebody answered." She hung up the phone.

"What did you hang up for?" Ida said.

"What was I supposed to say? Hello, this is Nina Fischman. Do you know who killed Mark Hirsch, by any chance?"

"You should have told them that you're encountering some legal difficulties in getting appointed as the executor of

Helen Hirsch's estate. And you need some additional information about Mark Hirsch in connection with some document that you have to submit to the court. Is there anyone there who could help you? Something like that."

Nina stifled the impulse to hand her mother the phone and say "You do it." It was an embarrassing impulse. She could see why people moved all the way to California just to avoid such situations. "All right. A woman answered the phone. Who do you think I reached?"

"Maybe one of his partners' home numbers."

"I guess so. It must have been the wife. I wish I at least had a name, for Chrissakes. Okay, here goes." Nina redialed the number. This time a kid picked up. "May I speak with your father?" she said.

"Who's this?" the girl asked.

"Nina Fischman." She looked at Ida and shrugged.

"Daddy, some lady's on the phone for you."

"Hello?" The voice was adult and male, but the tiniest bit high-pitched.

"Hello. My name is Nina Fischman." She could have sworn she heard a sharp intake of breath. She launched into her spiel, as choreographed by Ida.

"I see. Hold on one moment." She heard muffled voices in the background. "Perhaps this is a matter we should discuss in person. Could you come over here? I'll ask my partner Jerry Levinson to join us."

"Okay. How about tomorrow?" She might as well get this show on the road. Besides, she couldn't hold on to the rental car forever.

They made a late afternoon appointment and he gave her directions to his house in Kings Point. It was only after she got off the phone that she realized she still didn't know his name.

16 · · · · · · · · ·

Nina almost ran into the car in front of her, which had
stopped suddenly. She cursed the driver, a streaked blonde
presumably named Judy, since the silver Jaguar XJ6 had
JUDYSJAG as its license plate. This part of Great Neck bore little
resemblance to the neighborhood that the Hirsches lived in.
Beverly's house was in a postwar subdivision that could have
been anywhere. It was maybe a step above the little boxes of
Levittown, but not by much. Big boxes, really. But the houses
that Nina drove past on Tuesday night were not boxlike in
any way.

These homes had been built in the earlier part of the
century and had thick walls and thick foundations and thick
trees growing in their yards. Many had views of the water.
The streets curved around gracefully, flowing into each
other, obviating the need to make any mundane right or left
turns. This was clearly the Great Neck that the cabdriver had
referred to as the Promised Land.

Nina pulled up in front of 7 Woodcock Court. It was a

large white English colonial with two BMWs parked in the driveway. The white car had a CHILD ON BOARD sign affixed to the left rear window, one of the more objectionable cultural artifacts of the past decade. Wasn't an adult human life worth saving? And if it was the potential liability in a wrongful death action that you were worried about . . . well, shouldn't people ride around with signs that said things like thirty-four-year-old oral surgeon with lucrative practice on board? After all, those were the guys that cleaned up when it came to judgments in personal-injury suits. All those lost wages.

The punchline of a BMW joke came to mind. Break My Window. Nina stifled the impulse. The name on the mailbox was Silver, so it must have been Mr. Silver who opened the door.

"You must be Nina Fischman." His appearance matched his high-pitched voice. He wasn't exactly effeminate, but he looked soft. He was thin, but the kind of thin that comes from dieting, not from working out. Silver's body was narrow, with undeveloped musculature. The way people used to look in the sixties, when armholes were cut high up into your armpits and George Harrison and Mick Jagger were considered sex symbols, despite the fact that their combined weight was probably less than that of Arnold Schwarzenegger.

Silver was tall, in his mid-forties, and looked like he had just come home from the beauty parlor. Or hair salon or whatever they call it for men. But beauty parlor was what came to mind. Not only was his hair a suspiciously even shade of chestnut brown, but it had been blown into a perfect do that cascaded trendily but unintelligently down his neck to the middle of his collar. And Nina could swear he was wearing makeup. It could have been just overexposure at a local tanning salon, but she recognized that skillfully applied triangle of blush on the apple of his cheek. It looked almost natural. Almost. It was an effect that Nina had been trying to achieve her entire life.

He wore an expensive green patterned sweater, Missoni perhaps. She had never seen a man actually wearing one of those sweaters. Only Bill Cosby on television. Silver also wore jeans and suede Gucci loafers without socks. He extended his hand. The nails were buffed to a high sheen. Nina noticed an emerald cabochon pinkie ring and a big gold watch. "Steve Silver," he said. She shook his hand. "Let me take your coat." He hung it in the front hall closet. Nina caught a glimpse of shearlings and furs.

"Nice to meet you," she said.

"Come on in," he said without enthusiasm. He led her into the living room, where a somewhat older man sat on the couch. "This is my partner, Jerry Levinson." Levinson stood up and gave Nina a firmer handshake than Silver had.

Whoever had groomed Levinson had done a less impressive job than with Steve Silver. Jerry Levinson's hair was also suspiciously dark, but the eyebrows had not been dyed to match. They remained gray. The nails were not buffed, and despite his thinness he sported a small paunch. What was most noticeable about Levinson was his eyes. They were black, seemingly all pupil, and opened very wide. It made him look alert to the point of nervousness, like the nocturnal mammals in the Bronx Zoo.

Levinson's outfit was less striking than Silver's. He wore a basic navy-blue cable knit crewneck sweater, gray wool pants, and tasseled loafers. And socks. No jewelry except for a stainless steel watch. His voice was lower-pitched.

The room had been redecorated sometime since the Santa Fe craze hit. It was all of a piece, not as if someone had just added a Navajo rug here and a kachina doll there. They had done it from the guts on out.

A celadon and terra-cotta scheme prevailed, showing up

in the couch, the chairs, the rug, and the paintings. A Georgia O'Keeffe skull hung over the fireplace. An exhaustive pottery collection, with some important pieces, stood huddled together on the mantel. The vases looked related, like cousins. They might have been done by the same artist, or they were at least from the same pueblo. It was easy to picture Silver, touring around Taos in his BMW, stopping at a gallery and buying the place out.

The effect of the room was contrived. Nina couldn't help visualizing it in former incarnations—country French with Pierre Deux fabrics and Provençal jugs on the mantel, a dried topiary rosebush where the big organ-pipe cactus was now. Or in an Anglophiliac phase with chintz upholstery and a pair of ceramic King Charles spaniels bracketing the fireplace. You couldn't tell what had gone on before, since there wasn't a single leftover to clue you in.

What did these people do with their furnishings when the redecorating whim struck? They couldn't very well put everything into shopping bags and give it to the cleaning lady, could they? Maybe they did. Maybe somewhere down in Rosedale or over in Laurelton was an elderly black woman sitting in a Queen Anne chair with her feet resting on a little needlepoint footstool and with a three-dollar black folding umbrella nestled in a solid brass stand.

Silver joined Levinson on the couch. He motioned for Nina to sit down on a matching overstuffed chair. "Kathy," he called toward the kitchen. His wife instantly appeared, wearing an apron that matched the upholstery.

She appeared so instantly, Nina had a strong suspicion that Kathy had done a Lisa Hirsch, hiding in the hallway, listening. It was unnerving, this suburban business of people hiding in the hall. You couldn't do that in a Manhattan studio apartment.

"What can I get you?" she asked Nina, without being

introduced. The accent was still there, but all other vestiges of the Midwest had apparently been erased.

Nina looked closer. Despite the Adrien Arpel makeover, you could still see the faded outlines of a freckle-faced farm girl. Or maybe the daughter of a Kentucky coal miner who had run off after the war to work in the factories of Ypsilanti, Michigan. Or she could have been the daughter of a college-educated engineer who had chosen to raise his family in a suburb of Indianapolis. It was hard to tell. But what was clear was that this creature was not indigenous to Great Neck.

Where had Steve Silver found her? Nina pictured him as a college sophomore somewhere far away, overprivileged and arrogant, flirting with the townie waitress who had to work two jobs to supplement her scholarship. And then bringing her overseas, so to speak, to meet his parents. Who were thrilled on one level that their grandchildren might have a shot at such fine, delicate bones. But firm when it came to the importance of converting to Judaism.

They must have been persuasive, because Kathy had apparently converted in a big way. The nails were long and red and the fine light hair had been permed and sculpted into one of the bushy wedges favored by the modern American Jewess. Underneath the celadon and terra-cotta apron was a black jumpsuit, with the soft look of cashmere. And hanging from her neck was a *chai*. This piece of Judaica had the bright look of twenty-two-karat gold with a matte finish. Very Bergdorf Goodman. Was Robert Lee Morris doing a *chai* collection for Donna Karan?

Nina stared at the necklace and Kathy repeated her question. "Can I get you some coffee?"

Nina wondered if chocolate-amaretto beans was the house blend at the Silvers as well as the Hirsches. She didn't want to risk it. "Nothing, thanks. I'm fine."

Kathy Silver headed off in the direction from which

she'd come. Jerry Levinson leaned toward Nina, his elbows on his knees. "What was it you wanted to discuss? I'm not exactly clear about it. Something about Mark, Steve said."

Even without the gray eyebrows, his age would have been easy to place. Levinson was past fifty. His accent had the tones of a boyhood spent in a borough. A prewar borough, the Bronx or Brooklyn. Not a postwar borough like Queens. A boyhood spent in a borough listening to the radio and worrying about the war in Europe. He had a Woody Allen whine, unlike Silver's baby boomer accent, which was less Woody Allen, more Jerry Seinfeld. Silver's accent was shaped by Howdy Doody and Beaver Cleaver and schoolteachers who drove to work. A mere decade separated the birth of these two men. But a Jewish baby boy vintage 1937 was an entirely different product than the 1947 model.

Nina had been raised in a prewar borough. But she had been born in the fifties, and her accent was closer to Silver's. Her way of speaking had been battered down not only by Howdy Doody but by sleep-away camp and the Manhattan girls at Bronx Science and dormitory living. And, of course, by a schoolteacher mother.

Levinson's generation had missed a lot—drugs, premarital sex, campus life. But he must have enviable memories. Of a nation that fought on the right side, a subway system that could be safely ridden until all hours, a school system that educated you well and without charge all the way through college.

It was easy for Nina to sentimentalize. But she should remember that were she to be suddenly transported back to the Grand Concourse of 1942, she'd find herself trapped in a life without panty hose, air-conditioning, or career options. The best she could have hoped for was to "marry well." With her track record, she'd be somebody's old maid typist, wrestling with his correspondence without benefit of word processors or Xerox machines. The panty hose and air-conditioning maybe she could have lived without, but erasing the errors on the carbon copies would have done her in.

As Nina sat there, picturing some old bald guy yelling at her about her typing mistakes, Levinson cleared his throat in a way that indicated he expected an answer from her. She had to play this cautiously, laying out her cards one by one— and not let herself be intimidated. Well, Housing Court had been good for something. She had come a long way since law school, when all the women in her class uniformly began their recitations with "This might sound really stupid, but . . . ."

"Mark Hirsch was your business partner," she began. "Is that correct?"

Silver looked at Levinson, who answered by nodding.

"I'm the executor of his mother's estate. Mark had originally been named as executor and I was the alternate. But since he predeceased his mother, I had to step in. In preparing papers for the court, I've had to examine the circumstances surrounding his death. And I had a few questions that I thought you two could answer."

"Why don't you ask his wife?" Silver said.

"I've spoken to Mrs. Hirsch. However, there are some matters she has not been able to shed any light on."

"What do you want to know?" Levinson asked.

"Perhaps, for starters, you could describe the nature of your business to me."

Silver again. "What does that have to do with anything?"

She looked toward Levinson. He was turning into the judge, with Nina and Silver as opposing counsel. Levinson cooperated. "Steve and Mark and I formed a partnership some years back. HLS Associates. Our initials in alphabetical order. We started out doing real estate syndications, which was how we had met."

"The three of you met by investing in the same deal?"

"Not quite. Steve and I were both working for the same company. A fabric manufacturer."

"What company?"

"Silver Textiles." So that accounted for Steve Silver's overgrooming. He was a garmento.

"Your company?" she asked him.

"My father's." Even worse. A second-generation garmento.

"I knew Mark through some community activities that my wife was active in," Levinson continued. "We lived near each other."

"You live in Manhasset Hills?" she asked.

"Yeah." Things were becoming clearer. Silver was the one with the money. What Levinson brought to the package remained to be seen. "Mark was working for a couple of real estate syndicators that put investors together to acquire properties."

"When was this?"

"Eighty-two, eighty-three, around then. Anyway, Mark was raising money to buy a shopping center in Toronto. He approached me and I talked to Steve and we both decided to go ahead with the deal."

"So what happened?"

"We all made a lot of money." His face relaxed and his voice softened with the memory. "We got in just before real estate in Toronto took off. When our first check came in, the three of us went down to Atlantic City to celebrate. We all had really good luck at the blackjack table that night. We were riding very high. It was on the drive back that we started kicking around the idea of starting our own syndication company."

"Whose idea was it?"

"Levinson looked at Silver before he answered. "Mark's, I guess. He was looking to get out of where he was. The guys he was working for were father and son and he never stood a chance of being cut in as a full partner."

"What made the two of you decide to do it?"

"Mark was definitely talented. Even though he wasn't rich and didn't hang out with big money, he was remarkably good at finding investors."

"So he was the pitch man."

"Basically. We figured with his silver tongue and Steve's connections we could do really well."

"What was your contribution?"

"We needed Jerry," Silver said. "He's got a superb sense of how to run a business."

"Did you leave your father's place for this?"

"I was sick of chintz and brocade and all that crap. The idea of making money by touching nothing more than paper appealed to me."

"And did you?"

"Did I what?" Silver nibbled at a buffed nail.

"Make money. By touching paper."

"For a while."

Levinson broke in. "Initially HLS was very successful. But despite our abilities, we were not exempt from market conditions. Like everyone else in the real estate business, we hit upon hard times. The partnership was recently disbanded."

"Well, it would have to be, wouldn't it? With the death of Mark Hirsch?"

"Even before Mark died, we had pretty much wound down."

Nina decided to play a wild card. "Did Mark's drinking have anything to do with your business problems?"

Levinson and Silver exchanged glances. "His drinking?" There was obvious tension in Levinson's voice. "What do you mean?"

"Didn't Mark have an alcohol problem?"

"Mark wasn't a drinker."

"He didn't drink?"

"He wasn't a drinker."

"But did he drink at all?"

"He wasn't a drinker," Levinson repeated again. This was starting to sound like an Abbott and Costello routine.

"He was drunk when he was killed. Did you know that?"

Silver stood up. "Look, I don't know what information you're going after, but I'm telling you that we don't know anything about Mark's death. As I suggested, maybe you should contact Beverly."

Nina walked to the front hall closet and pulled out her coat. "I'll be in touch with both of you," she said, in what she hoped was a somewhat threatening manner. But then she ruined the effect by asking for directions back to the Long Island Expressway. And made it even worse by scribbling them down on the back of an announcement card for a shoe sale at Ecco that she had been carrying around in her purse for months.

17 . . . .

A car pulled up as Nina was walking out of the house. It had the sleek curved lines of something expensive. Never having been exposed to the cultural advantages of the suburbs, Nina wasn't too good at telling a Jaguar from a Porsche. But Mercedes-Benzes were easy, even for an automotive unsophisticate like her, since they had a prominent hood ornament that resembled a peace sign.

The driver, an older version of Steve Silver with broader shoulders and undyed silver hair, got out of the car and met her at the curb. He looked at her without disdain, but also without interest. The way rich people look at their Mexican maids in movies about California. She prepared to explain to him who she was and what she was doing there, but there seemed to be no need. All he said was, "Is Kathy in there?" and jerked his head the tiniest bit toward the house.

"Yeah, she's home."

"Hmm." He gave a small grunt of acknowledgment and walked past her.

"Are you Steve's father?" she called to his back, which was covered in a caramel leather jacket that looked like it cost upward of the annual GNP of Portugal. She had heard that Rolls-Royce seat covers were made from the hides of special cows, ones that had not been fenced in by barbed wire. So you got a smooth sweep of leather with no blemishes. If that was true, then this jacket could have come from the same herd.

"Yeah, Herb Silver," he said, without turning around.

"Pleased to meet you." This time he didn't bother answering.

He banged on the door and Kathy opened it. "How's my girl?" he boomed, and gave her a big hug and kiss.

"Fine, Dad." She looked responsive. Nina hung around watching until they both went inside.

Interesting, she thought as she got behind the wheel. Unusual for the shiksa wife and the garmento father-in-law to be so intimate. And for Herb Silver, rather than asking for his son or his grandchildren, to be asking for her. Well, Kathy wasn't walking around with an oversize *chai* hanging from her neck for nothing. She had obviously converted herself right into the bosom of Herb Silver.

She had called him Dad. It gave away her Christian roots, of course. Jewish girls continued to call their fathers Daddy until they were both in the nursing home. But it also revealed something else. That Kathy was playing by Herb Silver's rules and was getting something in return.

Nina started the car and headed back to the city as quickly as possible. The act of operating a motor vehicle was making her feel vulnerable instead of powerful; the cars zooming past her on the highway were unnerving. And she was only halfway through her menstrual cycle. At this rate, she'd be on the verge of a nervous breakdown in two weeks.

She passed exit 32, and Nina felt better being west of the

Nassau County line. Some people might find New York City to be fraught with peril, but the suburbs were starting to give her the creeps. They were so dark. Of course, now that someone had stolen a good portion of the copper wiring that kept the highway lights on, the city was not as bright as it used to be. But for the most part, you could see where you were going.

She wondered what the story was with those two. Steve Silver and Jerry Levinson had gone through the same evasive crap as Beverly. "He wasn't a drinker." And they had been exchanging looks just loaded with significance. Besides, Nina had to admit to herself that she hated Steve Silver on sight.

In the same way that Ida reacted viscerally to women in high heels, Nina was repelled by men without socks. Well, maybe if you were on an island off the coast of Maine in August you could get away with it. If you were wearing boat shoes, not Gucci loafers, and came from one of those families who considered a sailboat a family heirloom, not a bar mitzvah present. But for Steve Silver to be walking around Great Neck in February with Gucci loafers and no socks was unforgivable.

Nina had ridiculed her mother for basing her suspicion of Beverly on the height of her heels. At least Beverly had a motive. She had apparently blossomed after Mark's death. Her jewelry collection had, at any rate. Silver didn't seem to have a motive. Of course, passion can run high in business. Probably partners often feel like killing each other. Nina had heard partnership characterized as a marriage without love. And that was probably more true than ever in a business like HLS, with Chapter Eleven yapping at their heels. But even if Silver had felt like killing Hirsch, would he really have done so?

It was a mistake, Nina reminded herself, to confine her suspicions to someone just because he wore no socks. Levinson was probably the more dangerous of the two. He was a guy who had worked his way up. What had Steve said? That Jerry had a superb sense of how to run a business. Steve Silver was a natural follower, too soft to strike out on his own. Languishing in the shadow of his father, and then following Levinson off on a business venture with Hirsch, a guy he barely knew. He couldn't even answer any of Nina's questions without looking to Levinson for assent. Silver was definitely born to be someone's second in command.

Levinson, on the other hand, had leadership potential. His eyes were all pupil. He clearly took everything in. The talk of the *Science Times* this week had been a study that concluded that the saliva samples of male trial lawyers had higher levels of testosterone than male nontrial lawyers. Levinson was someone you could imagine in court. If you got both men to spit into a tube, it was a sure bet which was the one with testosterone poisoning.

And yet she could tolerate Jerry Levinson. Maybe because she could relate to him a bit. He still sported his borough accent and his nails remained unbuffed. He was probably hustling to pay the mortgage on his Manhasset Hills split-level. And if he dyed his hair she'd bet it was because Silver had told him it would look better to their clients.

Nina knew she was hypersensitive about men like Steve Silver. They held no interest for her, being vain and materialistic and shallow and of limited intelligence. Yet they always got to reject her first, before she got to reject them. It wasn't fair. They seemed to have some kind of radar that bounced back signals to them—watch out: chubby feminist ahead—before she even came into view.

So big deal. Who needed men like Steve Silver anyway? Let him rot in Nassau County with his two-manicure family and his Santa Fe pot holders.

As the Grand Central Parkway crested over Flushing

Meadow Park, she caught a glimpse of the Manhattan skyline. Nina felt the same tug at her heartstrings as always. Her romance with New York City was an old one and had its tarnished patches. Like any mate, the city had let her down over and over, thrown enough hard times her way. But like any good marriage, the scars receded into distant memory at times like these, when a crescent moon hung over the Chrysler Building and a silvery flurry of snow dusted the old Unisphere from the '64 World's Fair.

She renewed her vows with passion as she sped over the bridge. *Dear Lord, keep me away from places like Lake Placid, where I'd undoubtedly turn to drink, and Great Neck, where I'd probably be sticking my fingers down my throat like poor tortured little Lisa Hirsch.*

As she sped over the Triborough Bridge, Nina headed over to the right and guided the rental car into the Manhattan-bound traffic. Staying to the left led you to the Bronx, as everyone knew since the publication of *The Bonfire of the Vanities.* She objected to Tom Wolfe's portrayal of the Bronx on principle, but, like Sherman McCoy, she avoided the place whenever she could. Unfortunately, it was a pattern she had formed while still living there.

Suddenly the vehicle on her left cut sharply in front of her, some kind of shiny black skankmobile with a raised rear that looked like a duck's ass. The car missed clipping Nina's left headlight by a few inches.

It gave her the chills. What was she doing driving around like this anyway? She didn't belong behind the wheel, she thought. She belonged in her black Arche boots with the heavy rubber tread soles, trudging north and south along the avenues and east and west along the streets of Manhattan. Along with all the other smart though somewhat frustrated and ambivalent women with their suede boots and black leather Coach tote bags. Wearing earrings purchased at a crafts fair, not from some diamond dealer on Forty-seventh Street, and watches that disclosed the time, not your husband's net worth.

In fact, it was just fine with her if she never saw Beverly Hirsch again. Or Steve Silver or Jerry Levinson. Why was she investigating this murder anyway? She was the executor of Helen Hirsch's estate, not a private detective.

That was it, she'd made a decision. It didn't matter that it was only Tuesday and the car wasn't due back until Thursday morning. She was getting rid of it right now. Enough of this driving around and cross-examining people. She had been put on this earth to sit at a desk and answer the phone and draft legal documents. First thing tomorrow she'd start drafting letters testamentary for Helen Hirsch's estate.

18 . . . .

Nina practically skipped home from the rental garage, she was so relieved to be free of the car. It was one of those times when it all seemed right—her apartment, her job, the state of being carless and husbandless. The Upper West Side was at its wintry best; the Italianate brownstones were blanketed with just enough snow to show them off. Serious architecture for serious people who lived in a place with serious seasons. The homes had been built for upper-middle-class profession-als. And now, after decades of rooming houses and urban blight, housed them once again. Although both the large Vic-torian families and the large Victorian dwellings had in most cases been subdivided and redivided into smaller one- and two-person units.

Still, there was some lineage here. Nina's usual sense of alienation did one of its one-hundred-and-eighty-degree turns into a keen feeling of connection. She was the latest of a long line of legal practitioners to walk these streets with dig-nity.

The feeling faded a bit when she turned into her building, a tenementy affair that couldn't even pretend to be anything else. She stooped to pick up a bunch of Chinese take-out menus that someone had strewn all over the twenty-square-foot patch of linoleum that served as a lobby. By the time she had walked up the three flights of stairs and turned both keys in her two Medeco locks, she couldn't quite remember what she had thought she had in common with Benjamin Cardozo.

There was only one message on her answering machine. It was from Lisa. "Call me right away. My mother's not home. Oh, it's Tuesday night," she had added, as an afterthought. "A little bit after eight o'clock." She sounded nervous.

It was close to nine by now, but when Lisa picked up, she told Nina that Beverly was still out. "She went into the city with Stuart. They had tickets to Jackie Mason, so she won't be home until late. Something creepy just happened and I wanted to tell you about it."

"What happened?" Nina asked.

"I got a phone call from one of my dad's partners. Jerry Levinson. He told me to tell my mother to call him as soon as she could. And in the background I heard two people sort of yelling. And one of them mentioned your name."

"Well, that makes sense. I was just over at Steve Silver's house. He must have been telling his wife about me."

"What were you doing over there?"

"Trying to find out what happened to your father. Just like you told me to."

"You were?" Lisa's voice was filled with awe. Nina was immediately hooked. So much for dropping the investigation. That was short-lived.

"What did you find out?"

"Nothing much. Levinson and Silver were both very

closemouthed. Enough to make me suspicious. But I can't come up with a motive for them. What do you think?"

Lisa thought for a minute. "Meet me for lunch tomorrow," she said. "In the city."

Nina had to laugh. "I hadn't realized that you were one of the ladies who lunch. Who do you think you are, Jackie Onassis? Do you have a regular table at Le Cirque?"

"I'm serious," Lisa said.

"Don't you have to go to school? Aren't you still fifteen years old or have I missed something?"

"I'm supposed to go to a matinee tomorrow with my girlfriend and her mother. I could have lunch with you during the first act and meet them after intermission."

"And what are you going to tell your chaperon?"

"It doesn't matter. I'll tell her I'm having lunch with a friend from summer camp that I never get to see. She won't care. She'll hardly notice. If you think my mother's self-centered, you should see Mrs. Goodstein. Every time she takes me and Amber anywhere, she spends the whole time staring at herself in store windows. We could both get hit by a truck and someone would have to tap her on the shoulder and point to our bodies."

Apparently overprotective Jewish mothers had gone the way of the woolly mammoth. The next generation would be whining on their therapists' couches about an entirely different set of issues. "Okay," Nina said, "where should we meet?"

"How about Serendipity? Near Bloomingdale's."

Nina knew the place. They specialized in desserts. "No way. Frozen hot chocolate is not my idea of a proper lunch. But what else should I expect from a person who allows someone to fill their croissant with frozen yogurt? I'll meet you near the theater. What are you seeing?"

"*Cats.*"

"In that case missing the first act will be a blessing. Meet me in front of the Carnegie Deli at one-thirty. On Seventh Avenue near Fifty-fifth. West side of the street. I'll buy you some real food."

Nina worried about the excessive consumption of sweets by so many women. It had a misguided decadent edge to it, up there with women in high heels and men without socks. Not that she had a right to be self-righteous about any kind of food craziness, considering the weird shit she'd consumed over the years. Especially in the dorm, when marijuana had heightened everyone's sweets cravings and loosened their inhibitions. The years of French fries with honey. Then the sandwich of choice had been cream cheese and chocolate chips.

She really had no right to be judgmental. But Nina saw this socially acceptable practice of skipping the entree and heading straight for dessert in political terms. Real women ate real food. To pretend that you could exist solely on imported chocolate or the pastry basket at Bruce's was to deny that you were a human being who needed to be fueled up periodically.

The restaurant that Lisa had suggested was known for that sort of thing. Grown women, wealthy women who dropped all sorts of money on skin care and nutrition books and Williams Sonoma fish poachers, would march right in there and pretend that Death by Chocolate was a completely acceptable substitute for dinner.

As gin had been the cause of the sun setting on the British Empire, sugar might mean the downfall of the female middle class of Manhattan.

Lighten up, she told herself. Was the Carnegie Deli really any better? A place where they still pretended that it was normal for a sandwich to contain enough grams of fat to get you up Kilimanjaro. If gin had done in the Brits and sugar was doing in the ladies, then chicken schmaltz had single-

handedly decreased the life expectancy of an entire generation of Jewish men by a good ten years. And pastrami was
responsible for at least another five. But knowing Lisa, she'd
probably order cheesecake.

19 . . . .

Lisa ordered cheese blintzes. Something between food and dessert. They were lovely, with that same food-within-a-food quality as wontons. Nina ordered chicken soup with kreplach, a variation on wonton soup. As soon as it came, she immediately regretted not having a matzah ball. For an extra fifty cents, the waiter agreed to bring her one, and slipped it in among the kreplach.

Here she was, hitting ever-higher heights of ambivalence, torn between matzah balls and kreplach. As if in counterpoint, Lisa did a waffling little dance between applesauce and sour cream on her blintzes. She ended up with both, of course, just like Nina.

"So you met my father's partners," Lisa said, mixing her applesauce and sour cream into a mush and slathering it onto her blintzes. "What did you think?"

"Not exactly my type. Especially Steve Silver."

"He's the stupid one. Jerry's the smart one. Personally, I hate both of them."

"Why is that? Because they ran your father's business into the ground?"

"Nah. HLS would have gone down the tubes even if my father's partners hadn't been assholes. A business like that, there's no way it could have survived in this decade." Lisa used the phrase "down the tubes" with far more world-weary cynicism than was appropriate for her age. This was probably not healthy, but it made Nina proud in a way. Even if Lisa couldn't emotionally transcend a mother with a dressing disorder, at least she'd be able to tough-talk her way into making a living.

"A business like what? You mean real estate syndications?" Nina knew she wasn't using the term with familiarity.

Lisa gave her an appraising look, calculated to determine whether Nina needed the adult version, or the made-for-morons special edition. "Do you know what a private mortgage banker is?" she asked.

"No."

She continued to gaze levelly at Nina. "You're a lawyer, aren't you?" The question that was always bound to yield a disappointing answer. An answer that starts with *yes* and ends with *but*. Nina found the expectations enormous. The asker always expected her to be shrewd and knowledgeable in everything from criminology to finances to social work—while the truth was that she spent her days doing the same narrow little tasks over and over. Any sophistication she had about criminal law or investment strategy, she had gotten from reading the Sunday *Times*.

Nina gave Lisa a level look right back. "I'm a reasonably intelligent person. You don't have to oversimplify. I'll let you know if you're leaving me in the dust."

"Okay," Lisa said, finishing the last of her blintzes. Her eyes darted toward the rear of the restaurant, undoubtedly scoping out the ladies' room.

Uh-oh, thought Nina, here we go again. It was pathetic. Those three little blintzes were hardly worth throwing up. Not that anything was worth throwing up, Nina reminded herself. But those blintzes were so small.

Nina snapped her fingers for Lisa's attention. "Please begin," she commanded.

It worked. Lisa hesitated a moment and then started talking. Whew, Nina thought, close call. "You know what a mortgage is, don't you?" Lisa asked.

It wasn't such a ridiculous question in New York City, where a lot of the same people who couldn't operate a motor vehicle considered mortgages to be fabulous mythical beasts. After all, had anyone actually ever seen one?

"I know what a mortgage is. Although I've never had one of my own."

"Well," Lisa said, "when most people decide to buy a house, they go to a bank and apply for a mortgage. And the bank asks them for their tax returns in order to establish that they earn enough money to pay off the loan. Right?"

"Right."

"But let's say you have an all-cash business. And your tax returns show that you only made thirty thousand dollars last year. Actually, you took in two hundred thousand and you want to buy a house for half a million. The bank denies your application. What would you do then?"

"I give up."

"Go to HLS. A private mortgage banker. Instead of a *conventional* lender." Lisa spoke the word *conventional* as if she meant the smallest and narrowest of minds. "Of course, you would pay a price."

"What kind of price?" Nina had visions of broken kneecaps.

"Really high interest rates."

So they were usurers, Nina thought, like Isaac the moneylender in *Ivanhoe*.

"Not usurious rates," Lisa said, as though reading her mind. "State law permits up to twenty-four and a half percent. They never went above twenty-three."

Nina thought back to her own adolescence. She knew that she did not use terms like usury when she was fifteen. But she and her friends had their own vocabulary of sophisticated terms to show off. Maybe not that much had changed, except that teenage girls in the nineties threw around phrases like conventional lender instead of American imperialism.

"Did they make a lot of money as unconventional lenders?"

"Private mortgage bankers," Lisa corrected her. "You know, it's a real business. You have to be licensed and everything."

"I see."

"They made a lot of money for a while."

"Then what happened?"

"The real estate market got soft."

"And how did that affect them?"

"Take a typical borrower with a seven-hundred-thousand-dollar house. He put a hundred grand of his own money in, and he's paying twenty-two percent on the remaining six hundred thousand dollars. Suddenly the house is only worth half a million. What does he do?"

"I don't know. What does he do?"

"He walks away. And lets HLS foreclose. He'd rather do that than keep paying a six-hundred-thousand-dollar mortgage on a five-hundred-thousand-dollar house."

"But couldn't HLS go after them for the rest of the money by suing on the note?" That much Nina knew.

"The guy's showing twenty thousand on his tax returns. How are you going to enforce a judgment?"

Lisa obviously took great satisfaction in being smart. Nina understood the impulse, but also knew its dangers. It paralleled too closely Beverly's satisfaction in being thin. Both mother and daughter constantly monitored themselves. Smart was good for a longer run than thin. But even smart could come to an end. Nina sometimes felt her own level dropping, like estrogen, as she pushed toward middle age. There came a point when everyone lost their lead.

"Where did HLS get the money that they lent?" Nina asked.

"Good question. They did have a million-dollar line of credit from a conventional lender. That's a legal requirement, in order for you to get your license. But that doesn't go very far."

"Not when you're lending on half-million-dollar houses."

"Right. They already had a pool of investors lined up. From their real estate syndication deals."

"I see."

"How much do you know about real estate syndications?"

"Not much."

"I'll explain." Lisa looked pleased with herself, the way Beverly looked when she punched herself in the gut. "Let's say that you want to buy a hotel or a factory or a business. It looks like a great deal because the firm that owns it is going bankrupt and they're practically giving it away. You're sure that if only you could get the money together to buy it, it would throw off a huge profit. So what do you do?"

"I know one thing. You don't go to a *conventional* lender, do you?"

"And have to come up with the down payment and then have to pay points and interest? No way. You get together a group of investors who put up the money. Then they share in the profits. And you take your percentage off the top. That's what a syndication is. And when it's real estate that you're buying, it's a real estate syndication."

"I see. And that's how HLS started?"

"Right. My father worked for a real estate syndicator. Jerry and Steve were investors. Mainly Steve, I guess. He's the one with the money. His father's got a huge house on the water in Kings Point and Samantha Silver has her own horse."

"That's Steve's daughter?"

"Yeah. Not that I'd want a horse or anything."

"Of course not."

"No, really."

"I believe you." If there was one thing Nina didn't want either, it was a horse. She had never wanted a horse. There had probably been something askew about her preadolescence. She had managed to skip all the hallmarks of her latency period—horses, religion, tomboyism. And she couldn't remember feeling the least bit latent about anything.

"So anyway," Lisa continued, "the three of them started their own real estate syndication business and in the beginning most of the investors were Steve's relatives. I think they made a lot of money."

"So what happened?"

"The tax law changed. Real estate syndications used to be very desirable because they threw off huge tax benefits." Lisa narrowed her eyes. "I supposed you're not familiar with the concepts of active and passive loss?"

"I consider all my losses to be active ones."

Lisa ignored her. "When it became less profitable to invest in real estate, HLS started to get people to invest in mortgages instead."

"Was there a market for that sort of thing?"

"There's a market for anything that makes money." Lisa

was starting to sound a little condescending. "Anyway, some of the money was Steve's and some of it was his father's. But they also had outside investors. In fact, that's how my mother met Stuart Grossman."

"He invested with HLS?"

"Yup. The first time I ever saw him, he was in our living room, going over some investment stuff with my father."

"That's pretty interesting." Nina decided not to probe into how Grossman moved on from Mark to Beverly. "Why did Silver and Levinson describe themselves to me as real estate syndicators instead of private mortgage bankers?"

"The money-lending stuff can sound pretty tacky. The first thing it makes you think of is loan-sharking."

Jesus, this kid sounded more like a middle-aged accountant than a hysterical Jewish teenager with a mother problem. Well, times had changed. Security instruments were in, American imperialism was out.

Nina checked her watch. "I think it's time for you to get back for the second act."

"I just want to give you my theory."

"About what?"

"About my father's death."

"Okay, what's your theory?"

"Stuart Grossman killed my father."

"And why did he kill him?"

"I don't know."

"Every good murder theory has a motive," Nina said.

"Um, maybe Stuart lost a lot of money with HLS and blamed him."

"Is that a motive for murder? Or a lawsuit?"

"Maybe he killed my father so he could marry my mother. Or at least sleep with her. Although there's no evidence that he wasn't doing that even before my father died."

"Who do you think you are, Hamlet?"

"I'm perfectly serious," Lisa said, strapping her purse onto her shoulder.

Lisa could be on to something. After all, Claudius had been guilty of murder, with a little help from Gertrude. It was an age-old theme, this business of killing the father and sleeping with the mother. And Lisa did look like a modern-day Hamlet, all pale and tortured. Younger and chubbier, perhaps. But if Hamlet were alive today, Nina had no doubt he'd be female and bulimic.

"Okay, I'll think about it," Nina said as Lisa headed off in the direction of the Winter Garden Theater. Where *Cats* had been torturing audiences for almost a decade.

20 . . . .

The next day Nina took her usual route to the office while thinking her usual thoughts. She just couldn't decide which way to go on investigating Mark Hirsch's death. On the one hand, Lisa was counting on her to come up with the truth and there was something compelling about that. On the other hand, the thought of finishing up with Helen's estate—paying off the creditors, terminating the lease, distributing the assets, and washing her hands of the whole mess—well, there was something compelling about that also.

Nina was ambivalent. The way she was about whether or not to have kreplach, whether or not to have Tom Wilson, and so on, ad infinitum. Ad nauseam, to be more accurate.

But something unusual happened as she climbed up the stairs that led from the subway platform to the street. The same stairway she climbed almost every weekday morning. With the same grating in the sidewalk overhead. Suddenly, someone lifted up the grating out of the sidewalk and dropped two plastic crates on her head. Except that they fell on her foot instead. Not really even on her foot. One missed her entirely and the other landed near her foot, maybe a tiny bit on her toe. She couldn't really tell.

This was a new and different New York experience for Nina. And she thought she had had them all. The funny thing was that she knew immediately why someone had dropped a crate on her through the sidewalk grating—even though the woman three steps below her screamed "What the hell was that?" and the man with the briefcase at the top of the stairs turned to look at Nina with the crate on or near her toe and said, "I can't believe it." Well, Nina believed it.

It was as if she had mentally plugged into a Manhattan data bank and had successfully computed. She saw the answer in mental film clips—a three-card monte dealer quickly putting his cards in his pocket as a police car cruised to a halt, and throwing his crates, which he used as his gaming table, down through the grating to get rid of the evidence. Or it could have been an unlicensed street vendor chucking his display cases for the same reason.

"Are you hurt?" the woman behind her asked. The man with the briefcase had disappeared. It was always the women who tended to accident victims in the street. Men with briefcases were notorious not only for being unfeeling but for beating you out of subway seats and looking straight through the bellies of pregnant straphangers. Minority and blue-collar men were a little better, but the only men you could really count on all the time were the recent immigrants, who hadn't been here long enough to learn to ignore the needs of the millions of needy New Yorkers who surrounded anyone who ventured forth in this city.

"I'm okay," Nina told her, still trying to figure out whether the crate had hit her toe or was it just that the corn on her right foot was acting up again. It occurred to her that she should probably see a podiatrist. She'd been meaning to for a while. But for that matter, she should probably also see a pedicurist and a manicurist and a facialist and a masseuse and a colorist and a wardrobe consultant and a closet organizer and a personal trainer and a high-priced matchmaker that specialized in professional nonreligious Jews who were over thirty-five. And once she saw the podiatrist, she might not know where to stop. It was better not to even start.

"Have you ever seen anything like that before?" the woman asked her.

"No, but I'm not shocked." Nina went on to explain her theory about the three-card monte dealer and the unlicensed street vendor. The woman looked at her the way New Yorkers often look at each other. As if you were crazy but right.

By the end of the day, the incident had turned into a highly polished, highly amusing anecdote that Nina had added to her "I am a POW in NYC" collection. So by the time she reran it for her mother over the phone that night, it seemed a little threadbare.

"Where did you get that from?" Ida asked.

"Get what from?"

"That bit about the three-card monte dealer and the street vendor?"

"I intuited it," Nina said with pride. "It's something you just know when you've been knocking around as long as I have."

"Spare me the girl detective routine, will you? If you recall, your track record has been less than spectacular." Nina had to admit that she had been unable to spot last year's murderer in her own bed. But at least she had tried. "Did you actually see anyone suspicious when you came up to street level?" Ida asked.

"No," Nina admitted.

"Did you even look?"

"No," Nina further admitted. "I was on my way to work and in a hurry. Besides, I didn't want to get involved." That was the problem with sleuthing in New York City—you had to fight back an overwhelming impulse not to get involved. Tough turf for a yenta.

"I don't buy your theory," Ida said.

"Why not?"

"Because someone had to have dug up the sidewalk grating ahead of time. You can't lift anything that's been embedded in concrete without a lot of preparation."

"Well, the same guys probably hang around the same corner day after day, dealing cards or selling knockoff Louis Vuitton bags. And they probably get busted on a regular basis. It would be a worthwhile investment for them to dig up the grating."

"Come on," Ida said. "Can you honestly see some Senegalese street peddler coming in the middle of the night with a blowtorch? Give me a break."

Nina agreed that it seemed unlikely. "Maybe the grating had been loosened through some municipal snafu, a work order that had been issued and then lost. And the vendor noticed and took advantage of it. Making sure to peddle his wares within tossing distance of the grate."

"Oh, please."

"Ma, this is New York. Anything is possible. Keep in mind that I just got hit in the head with a plastic crate thrown through a subway grate. That, in and of itself, is farfetched."

"On the head? I thought you said toe."

"Hit on the toe sounds ridiculous. In the retelling, toe inevitably becomes head."

"Oy vey, now she's developing a veracity problem. I send my little peacenik to law school and she comes out Richard Nixon."

"I should be so lucky." Not that Nina would actually

trade places with him. Nixon was one of the few people she could think of who had a worse time in 1974 than she had. Losing your virginity to someone who never called you again was not as bad as being forced to resign from the presidency of the United States. Not really.

"Ready for my theory?" Ida asked.

"Keep 'em coming." Her mother's endless supply of theories could get tiresome, but deep down Nina enjoyed playing Yogi Berra to Ida's Whitey Ford. She was secretly proud of having a mother who could pitch straight into the strike zone. So many of her friends had mothers who threw mostly wild pitches aimed straight for the groin.

"Let me ask you something. Is this the same stairway you climb every morning on your way to work?"

"Yeah, unless I have to go to court."

"And do you get off the subway at the same time every day?"

"Pretty much. Within a five-minute range." If Nina had known that her life would be reduced to a five-minute range, she probably would have dropped out of law school and moved to the southern coast of Crete.

"Maybe someone was waiting for you."

"Who? Who was waiting for me?"

"Someone. Someone who wants to scare you into forgetting about Mark Hirsch's death."

"Don't be ridiculous."

"Why is it ridiculous? You yourself said that Beverly's boyfriend told you to keep your *shnozzola* out of other people's business. And those two business partners of Mark's don't sound, from your description, terribly gemütlich."

"Ma, you're making a big deal out of nothing. We live in a city where people lift up subway grates and drop crates on people's heads . . . um, toes, for no reason. It's just a fact of life."

"I refuse to believe it."

"Ma, you're a hopeless romantic."

"Yeah, right."

The funny thing was that she did consider her mother, who most people would put in the category of tough urban cynic, to be a hopeless romantic. Which did not reflect too well on Nina's own psyche.

"Well, what do you want me to do?" Nina asked.

"Why don't you phone your friend the cop and see what he thinks?"

She should never have told her mother that she had gone out with Detective Williams. "Ma, you know James is living in California now."

"So what's wrong with calling long distance?"

There was a suggestive tone in Ida's voice. Boy, things were really bad. Her own mother was proposing she attempt to renew a romance with a fifty-five-year-old retired black cop who lived on another coast. Nina considered offering up Tom Wilson to Ida, just to appease her. But she knew it would be a mistake. Nina hadn't heard from him since the morning of the jalapeño muffins.

She tried hard not to count how many days it had been, but couldn't resist the impulse. She knew that she and Tom had gone past the one-week danger mark. It was hard to admit, but maybe things hadn't gotten much better since 1974.

"Ma, I am not calling James Williams."

"Okay. But try and be a little bit careful."

"This from the woman who takes buses after midnight?"

"I don't know. It just kills me to take cabs crosstown," Ida said.

"So who told you to go to the East Side, anyway? It's not mentally healthy to spend time on the wrong side of the park. Too many women with skinny legs."

"That's ridiculous."

"Well, you have to at least admit that the heels are higher over there."

Nina knew that would get to her mother and she was right. "Yeah, I saw something you wouldn't believe last week on Lexington Avenue." And Ida was off and running with some anecdote about a leg cast and a purple suede pump.

21 ·······

After Ida hung up, Nina planned her evening at home. The term "evening at home" was not exactly accurate. In Nina's life, the concept had shrunk to a mere hour, hour and a half at the most. Since practicing law meant you couldn't leave the office before six at the absolute earliest, her major evening activities—aerobics and group therapy—could not be scheduled until seven. She was rarely home before nine.

To compensate, she relied heavily on quick-cooking dinners requiring little cleanup. Nina lived a life of ramen. An evening at home usually meant whatever sitcom occupied the nine-thirty slot.

On this particular evening, however, it seemed as though the networks had conspired to program an all-miniseries night, so Nina turned to other stimuli to entertain her. There were so many potential activities on her evening program, she didn't know where to start. There was panty hose washing and bill paying and phone call answering. All of which were commitments that were well past due.

No matter how hard she tried, she couldn't keep her obligations to a minimum. She never borrowed books from the library or rented videotapes, for example, because from the moment she put one of those suckers into her purse, she could hear them calling "Read me." "Watch me." "Hurry up before I'm overdue." It was too much pressure.

She also tried not to buy clothing that needed ironing, or to make any new friends. But despite her attempts to put a little Zen into her life, a dozen little duties yapped at her heels at any given moment.

Sometimes she thought about giving up the gym. She'd be free to go to the theater, maybe take an expensive course in something frivolous. Besides, she knew that aerobics was slowly doing in her lower back, even though she stuck to the low-impact stuff. By the time she was forty, she'd probably be dropping big bucks at a chiropractor. But she just couldn't stop.

Nina liked to think that she was not part of a cult. Not like Beverly, who had said "aerobics is my life," and meant it. Or like those women in the locker room at her gym who mourned deeply every missed class. And she knew she should be boning up on weight training, preparing for the day when she could no longer shuffle across the room with the rest of the pack. Judging by the way she was starting to feel, that day was probably close at hand.

The reason she couldn't give up aerobics was simple. It made you thinner. Nina knew that was the same reason that Lisa stuck her fingers down her throat. She wondered if her own approach was really less destructive.

Nina pulled out a pile of black panty hose to be washed. One of the blessings of winter was that you could wear black panty hose all the time and not have to sort them into little different-colored piles before you washed them. Also, they didn't get all stained at the heels the way lighter ones did. If she ever got rich, she'd take the money that other women might spend on jewels and furs and go for a new pair every morning, fresh out of the wrapper.

The phone rang. Nina resisted an impulse to let the machine kick in. She'd have to return the call eventually, and ignoring it now would just make her "to do" list longer. Not that she actually kept a list. She wasn't the list type.

She was continually amazed to see the array of writing implements and papers her friends the listmakers had—personalized notecards and fine-tipped felt markers and fountain pens filled with a rainbow of inks. Especially the ones who had gone to Mount Holyoke. Nina, with her public school education, used chewed up Bics and old envelopes and prided herself on her casually indecipherable handwriting—when she bothered to write anything down.

She forced herself toward the phone. Might as well get it over with. Unanswered phone calls weren't like unwashed black panty hose. You couldn't pile them all up and stick them into the same sinkful of suds and get them all answered at once.

"Hello?"

"Hi, it's Tom."

Nina was glad. For two reasons. First, he had called. Maybe things had improved since 1974 after all. Second, he had identified himself promptly. It was amazing how many people gave you just a "hi" to diagnose. It was a good way to spot the narcissists, as surefire as the Minnesota Multiphasic Personality Index.

"Tom, how are you?"

"Okay. Yourself?"

"Fine."

"I've been holding off on calling you," he said.

Uh-oh, Nina thought. Here it comes. Maybe a reconciliation with Chris or a new girl on the block. "How come?" she asked. She knew she sounded determinedly brave, while she would rather have sounded casual, but she couldn't help it.

"I waited until I got a chance to talk to Henry."

"Who's Henry?" Shit, Chris was one thing, but Henry was another. She hadn't seen this one coming.

"The police chief. The one I went to high school with."

"Oh, right. The police chief." Thank God.

"Not that I wanted to alienate Mel, by going over his head, but he's always focusing on playing by the rules."

"I know the syndrome." She had seen a lot of it, starting with Mrs. Kessler, her assistant principal who made them wear white shirts with little red neckerchiefs on Assembly Day every week. "Did Henry shed any light on Mark's death?"

"Not really. All these months have passed, so the physical evidence is gone."

"That's too bad."

"At first I thought we were getting somewhere. Henry remembered a similar incident that happened a couple of years ago. Some other guy drove over a cliff and his car caught on fire. They managed to pull his body out of the flames and did an autopsy. Turned out that he had been strangled to death before he went over the edge. The strangler had been counting on burning the evidence."

"Did they find the guy who did it?"

"Yup."

"And?"

"Turned out that it was his wife. And her boyfriend."

"Well, that doesn't help us, does it?"

"Not really. Interesting, though."

The conversation paused. Nina started to get a little nervous. Tom was starting to drop subjects and verbs from his sentences. Pretty soon he might stop talking. She pushed on. "I met Mark's business partners."

"And?"

"Not my type."

"But would they make good murderers?"

"I can't really say."

"What about his secretary?"

"Whose secretary?"

"Mark's secretary. Have you spoken to her yet?"

"I didn't think of it."

"Secretaries always know more of what's going on in the office than anyone else."

It was true. Nina knew that from personal experience. On the other side of the typewriter. She didn't have a secretary now, just a typing pool, so there was no one to know more than she about what was going on in her office. "Good idea," she said. "But how do I find her?"

"Ask the kid."

"Lisa. Of course." She'd call and see what she knew.

"Nina?" Tom paused. Nina bit her lower lip. "I just wanted to . . . um . . . say . . ." She could tell that he was having a hard time, but she stayed quiet and let him push himself. He deserved a little discomfort for the time that had elapsed before his phone call.

This calling thing was funny. She was not a big caller of men. Not that she subscribed to any sexist theory of female passivity. Nina had not led a life where men had come calling, filling up her dance card. Most relationships had been initiated by her. She found male aggression remarkably lacking outside of the courtroom. But once past the initiation phase, during that delicate period between the first and second date, she really did feel that men had an obligation to call.

Because they knew. They knew that they held her vulnerable little heart in their hands and it would just stop beating and dry up without proper attention.

So when it came to choosing a restaurant or a movie or picking up a check . . . well, she was right in there with them. But when it came to picking up the phone, she stepped back.

Her friends disagreed. They told her maybe she should call; men had all kinds of internal pressures of their own and would probably be glad to hear from her. She ignored the advice. The ones that didn't call in a timely fashion always ended up being more trouble than they were worth.

"I just wanted to say," Tom repeated, "that I'm sorry you live so far away." Pretty good. She gave him an *A* for effort. "After you left, I really missed you." Pretty good again. It would have been better if he could have brought himself to say that he had actually liked having her there. But missing her after she left was a close second.

"I missed you too," she said.

"I think we have something. Not like in law school, when we were just in a hormonal rage, but something more substantial. Meaningful. I feel like I can talk to you." Nina was touched. He had repackaged a somewhat disappointing sexual encounter into something more meaningful.

Meaningful. The other *M* word. That was good. He was a good repackager. The therapists called it reframing. And how did Nina feel about it? Mixed. She had, in the back of her mind, for all these years, been holding up that New Hampshire weekend as some kind of sexual standard. She had to admit it was disappointing to find that it would probably remain their personal best.

On the other hand, she agreed with him. Getting older meant looking for the less dramatic and longer lasting. The way she'd take a permanent fifteen-pound weight loss over a dramatic thirty-pound drop that wouldn't last the season. Or the way that Elizabeth Taylor had left her Richard Burton period behind and moved on to Larry Fortensky. Maybe old Larry didn't have Welsh poetry in his veins, but at least he didn't have a pint of gin flowing in them either.

"Can I come down and see you?" Tom asked.

"I'd like that."

"Chris is taking Annie to Disney World on the fifteenth of March. I could come for the weekend."

Nina did a quick calculation. She'd be just over her period, at her thinnest and least cranky. And the woman who cleaned her house every other week would be coming on the 13th. "Perfect," she said.

"Maybe I'll fly down and take a cab from LaGuardia. I'll call you when I figure out what time I'll get in."

"I can't wait," Nina said. As soon as she hung up, she reached into the refrigerator and threw the leftover kung pao shrimp into the garbage. If she stayed away from salt for the next couple of weeks, maybe her jawline would be visible by the time Tom arrived.

22

Donna Sabatini asked to be seated in the smoking section. Nina's heart sank, but she didn't object. After all, Donna was doing her a favor, giving up a lunch hour to talk about her ex-boss. She should be shown a little gratitude. So Nina wordlessly followed her as she threaded her way through tables of puffing diners and plopped herself down in their midst.

They were lunching at a midtown branch of Houlihan's —Donna's choice. Not that Nina minded Houlihan's, not the way she used to. Years ago, when she noticed that one had opened across from Lincoln Center, Nina predicted that it would fail. The food was adequate, but the atmosphere was freeze-dried. Like all chains, it had a characterless cuteness that conjured up images of network television and elevator music. New Yorkers would never go for it.

But after years of being worn down by the search for a Chinese chicken salad for under ten bucks and a clean bathroom, Nina found herself lunching at Houlihan's. Not frequently, but sometimes. Other New Yorkers must feel the same way, for the chain was sprouting up all over town. She suspected that for many Manhattanites, the term "character" had lost its connotation of nobility and had taken on a mild stench of urine.

"How did you get my phone number?" Donna asked, while reading her menu.

"It was on Mark's Rolodex, which was stored in his basement."

"And what were you doing in his basement?"

"I wasn't in his basement. Lisa found it for me."

Donna smiled when she mentioned Lisa's name. "That kid," she said. "She always did know everything." She took a cigarette from a pack of Virginia Slims and lit it.

Donna was small but curvy. And her curves were not hidden. She wore a tomato-red suit with a short tight skirt and a bolero jacket. Under the jacket was a black turtleneck with a high spandex content. Her long nails and high heels matched her red skirt.

"Did you know Mark's daughter well?" Lisa had been vague when Nina asked her about her father's secretary. She knew her name but not much else.

"Oh, no. We never met. Mark never let her near the snake pit." Donna leaned over to Nina and confidentially lowered her voice. "That's what Mark and I used to call the office." The "Mark and I" had a suspicious ring to it, as if it had been used over and over, as in "Mark and I spent our lunch hour in a hotel room."

"But Mark used to talk about her all the time," she continued. "He was crazy about her." Donna used her two-inch fingernails to flick back her dark brown hair. It was long except on top, like Melanie Griffith's friend in *Working Girl*. Donna leaned in even closer and more confidentially. "Mark told me everything," she said, in a way that furthered Nina's "Mark and I" suspicions.

"Ms. Sabatini," Nina began, "I've asked you to lunch because I need information. And, having been a secretary myself once, I understand how offices work. And who knows what's really going on." She decided to omit the fact that contacting Mark's secretary was a suggestion she had received from some secretary's male boss.

But Donna bought it. "Tell me about it," she moaned, rolling her eyes for emphasis.

The waiter came over, a young black man dressed in preppy attire. All the waiters and waitresses wore blue-and-white striped button-down oxford shirts and khaki pants. It was an interesting way to de-ethnicize a mostly minority staff. Even though the employees probably schlepped home on the A train to Bed Stuy every night, it gave the customers the impression that they were in a pleasant off-campus pub in Hanover, New Hampshire.

"What'll it be, ladies?" he asked.

Nina studied her menu. She decided that she wasn't enough of an optimist to order the Crab Rangoon. The probability of procuring a sufficient amount of real crabmeat in midtown Manhattan in this day and age for $6.95 seemed slight. She fell back on her usual Chinese chicken salad. She also ordered a club soda.

"Lemon or lime?" the waiter asked.

It was one of those hard questions in life that she could never answer. "Surprise me," she said.

Donna ordered something called 'shrooms, which seemed to be some sort of stuffed mushroom appetizer. Since when did people need cutesy names to entice them to eat? As far as Nina was concerned, the words "stuffed mushrooms" had sufficiently pleasant connotations to induce ingestion.

But that was the whole idea of Houlihan's. A meal there

was like an hour-long television commercial. Even the menu, a twenty-page magazinelike affair, carried advertisements. The concept that food was something to be consumed in a dignified manner had clearly been left in the dust. She momentarily wished herself in a small French bistro, where the mom-and-pop proprietors had lovingly and thoughtfully prepared the day's meal, which was written on a chalkboard.

But who was she kidding with this "food is holy" crap? It was that book she had read, *A Year in Provence*. She had better stay away from the sequel. If food was holy, why did she eat ramen for dinner every night? Besides, this wasn't the first time she'd eaten at Houlihan's and it wouldn't be the last. And she had to admit to actually reading those dopey articles like "Test Your Wine IQ" that filled the menu/magazine.

Donna stubbed out her cigarette and sat back. "What sort of information were you interested in?" she asked.

Nina hesitated. She didn't want to launch into anything prematurely. She felt that she hadn't established enough of a rapport with Donna to warrant asking difficult questions. She'd have to lay a little groundwork. "Tell me something about HLS Associates. For example, how did you come to work for Mark Hirsch?"

"Oh, I was just a kid." Donna still looked like a kid, maybe twenty-five at the most. "I had just graduated from high school."

"Which high school?" It was a question Nina could never resist.

"Lafayette."

"Bensonhurst, right?"

"Yeah. You from Brooklyn?"

"No, the Bronx. But I know Brooklyn pretty well. My sister lives there." Nina held back from specifying where, since Park Slope was one of those yuppie scum neighborhoods that people loved to hate. Folks who grew up in Bensonhurst differentiated between "brownstone Brooklyn" and the real thing. "Do you still live in Bensonhurst?"

"Yeah, I still live with my parents. But I'm finally getting married and moving out this summer. I've been engaged like forever."

Donna's hands were folded on her lap, away from sight, but Nina took a chance. "Let's see the ring." It was an easy bet, taking into account Bensonhurst and the long engagement. Besides, almost everyone had a diamond engagement ring lately. The most unexpected types—her punked-out young cousin; her formerly gay forty-five-year old colleague; even a law school friend who had spent an entire decade as a practicing Black Muslim.

Donna held out her hand with pride. The stone was round. All of a sudden, everyone's diamond was round. As Nina recalled, the elementary ed majors in her college dorm had spent a lot of time choosing between round, square, marquise, and pear-shaped. What had happened to all those nonround engagement rings people used to have? Were they somewhere in has-been heaven, along with Steve Silver's country French furniture?

"It's gorgeous," Nina said, although they all looked pretty much the same to her. Some were bigger, that was all. Just a woman's form of cocksmanship. The antique ones, however, could be pretty interesting.

"We're still paying it off."

"We?"

"Oh, yeah. Frankie and I have been putting both of our salaries in the bank for the wedding, so we put the ring on plastic, and pay for it out of our joint account." So much for the myth of the sheltered, cherished Italian woman who was kept on a pedestal and showered with gifts. Everything came out of a joint account these days. It was good to keep this in mind during the moments when Nina longed to be someone's financial dependent. It was like longing to be something extinct, like a brontosaurus or a pterodactyl.

"So tell me what it was like working for Mark."

"Well, like I said, I was just a kid when I started. Straight out of high school. I found my job through *The New York Times*."

"Really?" Most people that Nina knew found their jobs by snaking their way through a viper's nest of hideous gossip.

"Yeah, back in the days when you still looked under *G* for gal Friday."

It used to have such a snappy Rosalind Russell air to it. Of course, Nina had always known better.

"I think they hired me because I had been trained on the second-rate word processing system that Jerry Levinson's brother-in-law sold them. They decided they'd rather hire me, even though I cracked my gum into the phone, than have to figure out how to use their own word processors." Donna and Nina exchanged an "aren't men jerks" look.

"Which one did you work for?"

"At first I worked for all three of them, which was really the pits."

"Too much work?"

"No, there was no work when they were first starting out. But Steve Silver was having an affair with some woman who lived on Park Avenue, who Mark knew about but Jerry didn't. So I had to keep all that straight and cover for Steve a lot. Then he switched women and I had to fend off his wife and his ex-girlfriend and hide everything from Jerry. Finally, the business got going and they hired another secretary and I got to work exclusively for Mark."

"How was that?"

"We were a good match. Mark was a lot of fun. Of course, he could get out of hand."

The waiter arrived with their food. Donna's 'shrooms

were dainty. Nina's Chinese chicken salad looked huge. "Is that going to be enough for you?" she asked Donna. "Because you're welcome to have some of mine."

"Are you kidding? The whole point of coming here is the caramel nut crunch pie. This is just a warm-up."

"That sounds good."

"It is. They smash up Oreos and peanuts into the crust and fill it with ice cream and crushed Snickers bars. Then they cover it with caramel and hot fudge."

Uh-oh, thought Nina, not another one. She hoped this one stayed out of the bathroom. Maybe smoking was Donna's form of weight control. Keeping her metabolism up by dosing it with nicotine twenty times a day. Everyone seemed to have their own method, one worse than the next.

"What do you mean when you say that Mark could get out of hand?"

Donna got a funny look. Like the mushroom she had just bitten into had turned out to be a poisonous fungus. "I'll be right back. I've got to go to the ladies' room," she said, and bolted away from the table.

23 . . . .

It was a good sign, Donna running off to the ladies' room before she ate. A bulimic probably would have saved up her visits to the bathroom for after the meal. But Donna had looked awfully strange when she put the mushroom back on her plate after a tiny bite. Maybe she was anorexic.

So Nina was relieved when Donna returned, dove into her 'shrooms with gusto and gobbled them all up. Maybe she was a normal person who just happened to like cigarettes and sweets.

Nina was still chomping her way through her boring but dependable salad when the caramel nut crunch pie came. She let Donna work at it for a while, before she turned the topic back to Mark Hirsch. "You said that Mark could get out of hand," Nina reminded Donna gently. "What did you mean by that?"

"Why are you interested in all this, anyway? Mark's dead, the business has closed down, everything's over." She put her spoon back into her dessert and pulled out a Virginia

Slim. Nina considered requesting that she refrain from blowing smoke all over the table, but she didn't want to provoke Donna into running out on her again.

"I think that Mark died under suspicious circumstances," Nina said evenly.

"No shit, Sherlock." Donna lit her cigarette.

"So you agree?"

"One hundred percent."

"So why didn't you say anything?"

"To who?"

"To anyone," Nina said. "To the police, to Beverly, even to me when I called you."

Donna bit her lower lip and looked Nina straight in the eye. "Okay, here goes. Ready?"

"Uh-huh."

"Mark and I were in love. Everyone knew it." Nina must have looked shocked, because Donna shook her head. "We weren't having an affair," she added urgently. "We never had sex. Not that we hadn't discussed it. Mark was very gung-ho, always hinting that he might leave his wife for me and everything. But I knew it was bullshit."

"Why?"

"Beverly's a real piece of work. I didn't think he wanted to take her on. Besides, he adored Lisa. And worried about her. He wouldn't have wanted to put that girl through a divorce. And the bottom line was that Mark and Beverly, in some kind of crazy way, had a good marriage. They fought and complained all the time, of course. But I knew that neither of them was going anywhere."

"So you and Mark had a platonic relationship?" As soon as Nina used the word, it sounded funny to her. Rusty from years of disuse. It had been used to death in her youth, but now everyone seemed to either be married to or not speaking to each other. No one had time for the platonic middle ground.

But Donna knew what it meant. "Platonic?" she said. "No way. It was the most sexually charged relationship I've ever had. Sometimes I think that staying out of the bedroom is the ultimate aphrodisiac."

"Abstinence makes the heart grow fonder," Nina said off the top of her head. Dorothy Parker had nothing on her. Although Houlihan's was hardly the Algonquin and Donna Sabatini wasn't exactly George S. Kaufman.

"Maybe that's the real reason I wouldn't sleep with him. I was afraid it would ruin it. But I like to think that I held off because of Frankie."

My God, thought Nina, could this spunky, curvy little thing be a virgin?

"I know myself pretty well," Donna went on. "And I know damn well that I'd be much happier married to a New York City sanitation worker, with a house on Staten Island and three kids, than spending my life with Mark, listening to him complain about alimony and visitation rights. No matter how much money he made. And I knew that if Frankie ever found out that I had slept with Mark, he'd walk out on me. So Mark and I restrained ourselves." This time "Mark and I" had a more wistful ring to it.

"Was his death very painful for you?"

"Of course. But in a way it was a relief. I was at the point where I couldn't stand seeing him anymore, but I couldn't get myself to leave the office either. I guess you could say that I was addicted."

"Did your fiancé know this?"

"He was insanely jealous of Mark. To the point where it was ruining our sex life."

So much for Nina's virgin theory. The whole whore/madonna syndrome seemed to be crumbling. Even Italian girls from Bensonhurst slept with their boyfriends and paid for half of their engagement rings.

"Frankie was always trying to get me to quit my job."

Nina got a sudden image of a crazed garbageman stuffing a body into the back of his truck. Or maybe Donna had done Mark in. She had admitted that she was addicted to him. Maybe murder was the only way to break the addiction.

Or Frankie and Donna could have done it as a team, she luring Mark off for a secluded weekend, promising finally to deliver, and Frankie pushing him off a cliff.

Maybe Beverly and Stuart had been in on it too. After all, weren't Frankie and Stuart in the same business? The disposal business. Maybe everyone had conspired in the disposal of Mark Hirsch.

Or maybe Nina was getting a little carried away.

"So you were also suspicious about Mark's being drunk when he died?" Nina asked.

"Drunk? What are you talking about? Mark never drank. He was a diabetic." Donna looked genuinely shocked.

"He was drunk when he went over the side of the road. It was in the accident report."

"Bullshit."

"You didn't know?"

"How could I have known? The whole thing was hushed up. Steve and Jerry whispering in the office for about a day, then Jerry taking me out to lunch and telling me 'Mark's dead' when the check came. And sending me home for the week. That was all, just 'Mark's dead.' And when I asked him about it, all I could get out of Jerry was 'car accident,' that was all. And no funeral, just a private cremation without a memorial service. And Beverly was completely monosyllabic when I called her. She said she was in a state of shock and couldn't talk. I figured at the time that she didn't want to talk because she knew that Mark had been in love with me."

"Is that what made you suspicious about Mark's death?"

"I was suspicious even before he died."

"About what?"

"Look," Donna said, "I don't know who you talked to about what, but I'll tell you something." She paused.

"What's that?" Nina prompted.

"They're all lying to you."

"What do you mean?"

Donna looked at her watch. "Time to go back to work."

"Come on, you can't leave me hanging after a line like that."

"But I'll be late. And I don't want to piss my boss off. It's a good gig, a fancy law firm with a fancy salary. Definitely a step up from HLS."

"Can I at least walk you back to your office?" Nina doubted that Donna, with her short legs and high heels, could keep up too fast a pace. She'd have time for at least a short cross-examination.

"Sure."

Nina got the check, paid it, and followed Donna out of the restaurant. She was wrong about the pace. It was amazing how quickly some women could move on those things. They were at Donna's building before Nina knew it.

Donna put a hand on the revolving door to enter the lobby. Nina put her hand over it. "Just tell me one thing," she said. "What made you suspicious?"

Donna removed her hand from the door and turned to face Nina. "Look," she said, "I'd like to wipe out all memories of that period of my life. Meeting Mark Hirsch was probably the worst thing that could have happened to me. Now I'm finally forgetting about him and getting my life together. The last thing I want to do is jeopardize my future by opening up a lot of old wounds."

"I understand that. But I've stuck my nose far enough

into this to figure out that Mark was probably murdered. Can
you just walk away from that?"

"I can try." Donna sighed. "Mark felt that he was in danger. That's why he disappeared."

"Why was he in danger? Who was he afraid of?"

"There was a lot of shit going down around him. A lot. I
probably don't even know the half of it. He confided in me,
but only up to a point. I think he stopped himself from telling
me everything in order to protect me." Donna looked at her
watch again. "I've really got to go."

"Can I meet you after work? For a drink?"

"I can't tonight. Frankie and I have to listen to a band.
For the wedding."

"What about tomorrow?"

"Give me some time to think about this. I'll call you."

"When?" Nina asked.

"When I'm ready."

"I could call you instead."

Donna put her hand back on the revolving door. "No,"
she said. "Don't call me. I'll call you when I'm ready. I promise."

Nina pulled a piece of paper out of her pocket and a pen
out of her purse. It turned out to be a bank deposit slip, but
she used it anyway to write her office and home phone numbers. She pressed the slip into Donna's hand. "Please call
me," Nina told her.

Donna took the paper, revolved herself into the lobby,
and was gone.

24 . . . .

Mother and daughter were eating skinless chicken in a skin-
less chicken emporium on Broadway later that evening. The
days of extra crispy were clearly over. Skin had become a
four-letter word. Instead of cole slaw and potato salad with
your skinless chicken, you got more highly evolved side
dishes like cracked bulgur and lentil salad. It actually all
tasted quite good, creating the illusion that a life without skin
was worth living.

Dinner was Nina's second skinless chicken meal of the
day, coming on the heels of her lunch at Houlihan's. It was
putting her in a bad mood. Ida pushed a lock of hair off
Nina's face. The gesture worried her daughter. Ida had been
doing a little too much of it lately.

Of course, Ida had spent Nina's childhood trying to get
the kid's hair off her face. It had been an unruly mop and all
of the cute barrettes made for little girls could hold back only
a small segment of Nina's thick hair. This had been a source
of great concern for Nina, back in the age of thin, blond, and

straight. Later on, there were irons and CurlFree and jumbo rollers to straighten out the kink, but it had always been too thick to fit into any commercially available hair implement.

And then along came Janis Joplin to encourage the frizz. She was encouraging in many ways, an unconventional ugly duckling who refused to pay homage to thin, blond, and straight. Janis stressed volume, in hair and voice, and made Nina feel better about everything. She made a lot of women feel like they could give up another piece of their heart without bleeding to death. It was about this time that Ida stopped pushing Nina's hair out of her face.

Janis had been wrong about not bleeding to death, but Nina remained firmly committed to "more is more." More hair, more volume, more of everything. She worked hard at becoming someone not to be messed at. And Ida had kept her hands off until lately. Nina knew it was directly proportional to her vulnerability, which had taken an upward turn when her thirty-fifth birthday had coincided with ending a long-term relationship. So whenever Ida's hands crept back onto her hair, it was an upsetting reminder that something was wrong.

Ida wasn't the only one to indulge. Women she hardly knew, older ones usually, would tell her to get her hair out of her face and sometimes give her forelock a flick. The worst was when they added that deadly comment—such a pretty face. Because Nina was sensitive about her face. She was sensitive about her face because she was sensitive about her body. "Such a pretty face" was, she knew, a kindly way of telling her to do something to make her body catch up, yet another euphemism for "Why don't you lose weight?"

She always figured herself to be hypersensitive, maybe imagining this. Until she stumbled upon a book entitled *Such a Pretty Face: Being Overweight in America*. The book revealed that throughout the country, chubby young women were having their hair pushed back and being told in tones that blended blame and pity that they had such a pretty face.

Of course, her mother knew better than to speak those words. But sometimes she just couldn't keep her hands off.

Ida leaned across the table and pushed another lock of hair off Nina's face. Nina swatted her hand away. "What's the matter?" Ida asked.

Nina decided to launch into it. "It's Mark Hirsch's secretary."

"What about her?"

"I had lunch with her today and I can't figure her out. She's about twenty-five, worked for Mark since high school. She seems to know quite a bit, that there was a lot of shit going down around Mark, but she won't tell me what. At least not until she thinks about it some more."

"What is there to think about?"

"Plenty. For one thing, apparently Mark and she were in love."

"Mark was having an affair with his secretary?"

"No, not an affair. She says that they were in love, but never had sex."

"Do you believe her?"

"It never occurred to me not to believe her. Why would she lie about it?"

"If they were having an affair, why would she tell the truth about it? Mark's dead, now no one need know."

"True." Nina shook her head in agreement.

"Did she seem like she was telling the truth?"

"I couldn't get a read on her. She was unusual. In some ways she was just a regular kid from Bensonhurst. With her manicure and cigarettes and *Working Girl* hairdo. But she was articulate, and had a self-awareness that you just don't find in people with her background."

"Watch the stereotyping," Ida said sharply.

"Ma, I know you think that I'm just giving you the snotty Jewish girl routine, but drop the banner of liberalism and listen for a minute. People generally act certain ways depending on where they come from. And when they don't, it's worth noticing. Pretending that there are no such things as cultural patterns is denial. Besides, that way you miss the exceptions, which are the truly wonderful parts of life."

Ida remained silent. It made Nina feel guilty. She knew that her mother had struggled hard to buy her daughter the luxury of being able to focus on the wonderful exceptions. The solidarity of the first half of the century had paid the tab for the bourgeois individualism of the second half.

"Anyway," Nina continued, "she told me that she was extremely suspicious, even before Mark died, but she kept her mouth shut."

"How come?"

"She said she wanted to forget about Mark and that whole part of her life, to put it behind her. She's engaged to some garbageman named Frankie."

"Oh, really?"

"You sound a little dubious, Ma."

"Nina, you've been through a few relationships with men over the years, haven't you?"

"A few," Nina said cautiously. To Ida, Nina's dozen or so boyfriends must seem like a lot. But she had friends who could count up into the triple digits. And Wilt Chamberlain had just written an autobiography in which he claimed that he had slept with twenty thousand women. Nina had seen him on television, pitching his book. The interviewer had done a quick calculation and pointed out that over his lifetime that averaged out to more than a woman and a half a day. Wilt just nodded.

"A few," Nina repeated.

"And when you're trying to get over someone, is the

method you generally employ one of keeping quiet and just forgetting about him?"

"No," Nina admitted reluctantly. The method she generally employed was one of obsessing and obsessing, often out loud, until she got sick of the entire subject. "But Donna Sabatini might be different. Just what are you trying to say?"

"That there might be other reasons why she's keeping quiet. Maybe she's covering something up."

"I really don't think so."

"But she may be covering up for someone else," Ida said. "Maybe the garbageman."

"It's possible."

"Or Beverly."

"Oh, Ma, you've been subscribing to the widow with a smoking gun theory from the beginning. And it's all because of her high heels, isn't it?"

"It's not just the high heels. Talk about motive, she's got a big one. And as far as opportunity goes, didn't you tell me that the private investigator she hired found Mark for her? And then a few days later he died. That's a pretty big coincidence, isn't it?"

"Pretty big. Maybe Donna is covering up for Beverly. She told me that one of the reasons she never slept with Mark is that if her fiancé found out he would walk out on her for good."

Ida nodded. "So if she did have an affair with Mark and Beverly knew about it, then Donna would be afraid to go pointing any fingers at Beverly, wouldn't she?"

"I guess so."

"Or maybe," Ida said, "the only people who knew about the affair were the people in the office. And someone killed Mark for some business reason and Donna's afraid to say anything."

"But what kind of business reason? I mean, it's not like

they were international gem smugglers or something. At worst, they were boring white-collar criminals. People don't get killed for charging too high an interest rate."

"I don't know. You met Silver and Levinson. Do they seem capable of murder?"

Nina thought about it. "I can't tell. It's hard for me to be objective. The way you feel about Beverly's high heels, I feel about Steve Silver and his buffed nails and no socks."

"What about Levinson?"

"Again, it's hard to tell. I didn't mind him, sort of liked him. But that might only be in comparison to Silver. If I got him alone, I might find him to be an odious creature."

"So what's your next move?"

"I don't know. I'm dying to talk to Donna again. I wish I could think of some way to convince her to come clean."

"Why don't you bribe her?"

"Are you kidding?"

"I'm serious," Ida said. "I don't mean that you have to slip her a thousand bucks in an envelope in small bills. Butter her up, send her a little token of your appreciation, thanking her for her time."

"Good idea." Sending notes and cards weren't things that came naturally to Nina. Not that she wasn't thoughtful. She was usually full of thoughts, but never thoughts of sending things to people.

"Do you have her home address?"

"Yeah. Lisa read it to me from Mark's Rolodex. But what kind of token should I send her?"

"I don't know. You're the one who met her. What do you think she would like?"

"Hmm." Nina was puzzled. Then the answer came to her. "You know, Ma, more than anything else I think that Donna Sabatini would like a box of chocolates."

25 . . . .

Nina never had a chance to get to Godiva. Donna called her the next morning, from the office. "Want to have lunch again?" she asked Nina.

"Absolutely." Nina was thrilled. "You pick the place. My treat."

"Actually, I brought my lunch today. Want to go to my law firm's cafeteria? It's nice. That's where I usually go when I bring my lunch."

"Sure. What time?"

Donna hesitated. "Now that I think of it, I'd rather go someplace private. I'll get a conference room here, if that's okay with you."

"Whatever you say. I'll pick up a sandwich. Just tell me when and where."

Donna gave her the name of a big, well-known law firm. "You've heard of them?" she asked.

"Sure. But I thought they were on Park," Nina said.

"They moved last year." Donna explained. "Part of the Times Square Redevelopment Plan."

"How is it over there?"

"You were here yesterday. What did you think?"

"I was too distracted to notice."

"Well, take my word for it. It's gross."

It *was* gross, Nina had to agree that afternoon, looking out the window from the M104 bus. The homeless in the West Forties and Fifties made the homeless in the rest of the city look like people living in genteel poverty. There were a large number of canes, crutches, and stumps. Many seemed incapable of remaining upright.

It was a shame, thought Nina, as she picked her way through the human debris, that so many out-of-town tourists chose to spend time in this neighborhood. They were evident in great numbers today, clad in acid-washed jeans and snow-white running shoes, clutching their maps and staring in terror. No wonder the national impression of New York City was one of a chamber of horrors.

But Nina had to admit that it was amusing to think of all those high-priced attorneys in Donna's law firm, some of the world's most privileged, torn away from their tony gyms and clubs on the East Side, plunked down in the middle of the world's most needy. An ironic scenario. You bust your balls as an undergrad, take the Stanley Kaplan LSAT prep course at least once, somehow get into a highly ranked law school, claw your way onto *Law Review*, sweat out a couple of seasons as a summer associate, being charming and diligent without a break.

And your grand reward is a job in a neighborhood worse than the one your immigrant grandmother lived in. You're forced to share sidewalk space with hordes of bums and doomed to order out lunch for the rest of your working days.

It made the starting salary of eighty grand look decidedly less desirable.

Donna's law firm wasn't the only one that had taken advantage of the lower rents and moved westward. Nina didn't exactly run in those circles, but she had heard tell of recent law grads refusing to work for West Side firms. In her day, no one had to pick their employers by their zip codes. Fancy was fancy.

The street was grungy, but the building was brand-new. She had hardly noticed it yesterday, when she had walked Donna back after lunch. The lobby was awesome, with huge ceilings and lots of marble. It had a Mussolini feeling to it.

The reception area on the thirty-eighth floor was even more impressive than the lobby. Postmodern, with verdigris copper sconces and plaster faux Roman ruins serving as end tables. They must have left the Chippendale back on Park Avenue.

She thought of Steve Silver's Santa Fe living room. There's gotta be a way to get your hands on the castoffs, Nina thought. Did they sell them in the thrift shops? She'd definitely be interested. She supposed that was as close as one came to upward mobility in the Fischman family, moving on to the resale shops instead of snatching potluck from the compactor room.

The receptionist was as polished as the decor. Her suit and hair were both perfectly cut. Nina wondered how much they paid this woman to sit at the bird's-eye maple desk and operate the phone console. Clearly enough to afford couture. Or maybe they paid her a crummy wage and made her wear last year's fashions, handed down by the partners' wives.

Nina had a friend who worked for a firm like this. Her name was Joyce and she made a shitload of money. At times, usually during a bad day in Housing Court, Nina tried to picture herself in Joyce's shoes. Would she be happier?

Maybe she'd made a mistake, choosing the path she did. But then Joyce would complain about something, like having to stay up all night three days in a row, or being banned from playing tennis at the annual firm outing because she wasn't wearing all white. And Nina would have to admit to herself that she might as well be considering a move to another solar system.

The perfectly cut receptionist buzzed Donna, who immediately appeared. Today her outfit was pink, the suit still tight and the heels still high. The nails had been repolished to match. This was a more complex feat than one might think, since it meant she had to pick out her outfit and do her nails the night before, unless she got up at five o'clock in the morning to give herself a predawn manicure. Nina wondered how many times a week Donna did this. And whether it could be good for her nails.

She led Nina into a conference room with suede-looking walls. A large marble table dominated the space. Hung around the room were details of architectural plans framed in burled walnut. Nina wondered whatever happened to those corny Daumier prints they used to have in law firms, the ones with the caricatures of the grotesque attorneys. It seemed to be in bad taste to give any hint that you were in a law firm these days. Better that people should think you were in an advertising agency or a bank. Someplace respectable. The profession had never recovered from Richard Nixon.

"Nice joint," Nina said as they sat in chairs that matched the walls.

"It's not as cozy as things were over at HLS, but there's something to be said for that, I guess. We were all a little too close for comfort." Donna fanned herself with her hand to show what she meant.

"Ms. Sabatini—" Nina began.

"You can call me Donna," she cut in. "Although I appreciate the courtesy. It's not often extended to a secretary."

"It doesn't get much better when you become a lawyer. It's always 'Nina,' though they have stopped calling me 'honey.' I guess the three years and ten thousand dollars in student loans were worth it."

"C'mon. You don't want to spend your life answering someone else's phone, do you?"

"You're right. That's the worst. Do you plan to spend your life that way?"

"Who knows?"

"You could probably do pretty well for yourself in the right situation."

"Mark helped me a lot."

"Give yourself some credit. You're obviously a smart woman. Mark's not responsible for that."

"Yeah, I was always smart, but not polished." Obviously, she was not referring to her nails. "Know what I mean? Mark was a genuinely talented talker. I guess I started aping him. My family tells me that I talk like a Jew."

"It's better than cooking like a Jew."

"I guess. Although they do make better cheesecake than Italians, in my opinion."

Nina steered the conversation away from dessert. "Donna, you said, and I quote, that there was a lot of shit going down around Mark. What did you mean?"

Donna leaned back and chewed on a fingernail, thinking. Actually, she sucked on a fingernail. Chewing would have done too much damage. "For one thing," she began, "the business was falling apart. It wasn't their fault. The entire real estate industry had gone down the tubes. They were victims of a soft market." She did talk like a Jew. She reminded Nina of Lisa. Funny, the fifteen-year-old and the Italian secretary both sounded like middle-aged Jews, while Beverly sounded like an adolescent.

"HLS had entered into a ten-year lease," Donna continued, "for a whole floor in a Madison Avenue building. Actually, the entrance was on Fifty-fifth Street, but it had a Madison Avenue address. To impress the investors. They had fixed the place up to look like they were using all the space, but in reality, they rented the back half to other guys who had small businesses. Accountants, real estate brokers, guys like that. They didn't give them leases, since HLS figured they'd grow into the space. This was in the mid-eighties when everyone thought that growth was something that could go on forever."

"I recall that public sentiment." Nina had never shared it, being one of the youngest Americans who maintained a Depression mentality.

"Anyway, they did okay for a while. Jerry sent his kids to college, Steve's wife redecorated a couple of times, Beverly added to her jewelry collection."

"And then?"

"Everything started to crumble. As I said, it wasn't their fault. The same thing was happening to everyone else in the business. The little guys in the back rooms were also having a hard time. The recession was hitting them too. Most of them had to give up their space, which meant that HLS's overhead was higher than ever."

"And they couldn't rerent the back offices?"

"It had become a tenants' market. Renters were hard to find. HLS tried to get out of the lease, but the landlord was apparently playing hardball. That's when Mark started getting paranoid."

"How come?"

"He told me that there was a provision in their rental agreement that the lease could be terminated upon the death of a managing partner. And guess who was the managing partner of HLS?"

"Mark Hirsch?"

"You got it."

"So Mark thought that his business partners were going to kill him to get out of their lease? I would find that pretty upsetting."

"Jerry had told him to be careful, to get out of town for a while."

"So it must have been Steve Silver," Nina said.

"I guess, but I can't quite buy it. Sure, Steve could be a real shithead, especially with women. He was a chronic cheat, and whenever Mark wasn't around he'd hit on me unmercifully. I certainly wouldn't trust him with my little sister."

"And in business?"

"A real asshole, always trying to put the screws on everyone, squeezing more and more money out of the investors, even after he knew a deal wasn't going to pay out."

"But not capable of murder?"

"Not of murdering Mark."

"Why not?"

"Steve loved Mark. Not like I did; I don't mean to imply anything sexual. But Steve worshipped him. He hasn't been the same since Mark died. He's still in mourning, as far as I can tell. Though, believe me, I haven't wanted to get too close."

"Are you sure it's not guilt that Steve's carrying around with him?"

"Could be. But I'd be really surprised."

"I see."

Donna checked her watch and then looked at their still-wrapped lunches on the marble conference table. "We forgot to eat our lunch," she said.

"My God, I haven't forgotten to eat a meal in quite a few decades."

"Yeah, well, I figured you'd be sort of interested in what I had to say."

"Interested is an understatement," Nina said.

"We better eat. I've got to get back to my desk soon."

"Okay."

Nina unwrapped her tuna salad on rye. Donna had brought what seemed to be the leftovers from a major family feast. Out of the plastic wrap and tinfoil came stuffed rolled beef, a large wedge of some sort of frittata, manicotti sliced in bite-sized pieces, and something home-baked studded with candied fruits.

"My God," Nina said, "do you eat like this every day?"

"I've got a mother and a bunch of aunts that just hang around cooking all the time. Maybe that's why I still haven't gotten married yet. I don't want to give up all this food."

At least the woman had a decent excuse, Nina thought, biting into her pallid tuna salad. She wished she could come up with one too.

26 . . . .

Was Donna lying? Did she and Frankie push Mark right over the edge and then make up that whole business about death of the managing partner? Was Donna Sabatini capable of such a fabrication?

There was one way to check. As soon as they left the conference room, Nina headed east, over to Madison, then up to Fifty-fifth Street. On the southeast corner there was a white brick building, 545 Madison, with an entrance on the side street. Nina entered the lobby and took a look around. It was an ordinary postwar office building. She checked the directory. HLS was no longer listed. Mounted near the elevator bank was a wall plaque. She stepped up to read it. It indicated that the building was managed by the firm of Star and Wood, one of the bigger commercial real estate management firms in New York.

Nina scurried westward again, back to her office. When she arrived, she couldn't help but contrast her office building with 545 Madison. Hers was near Columbus Circle, in a fringe neighborhood that qualified as neither midtown nor the Upper West Side. It had that dumpy not-for-profit look. There was no plaque next to the elevator and judging by the condition of the lobby, she would say that it was managed by nobody. The elevator inspection certificate had been graffi-tied over.

Nina dodged the thick stack of phone messages that the receptionist waved at her, and grabbed the Manhattan White Pages. Her experience with managing agents had been lim-ited to Housing Court, where employees were sometimes sent by the landlord in eviction proceedings. She was used to us-ing an adversarial tone with them. She'd have to remember to cool it.

Star and Wood's phone listing was for a general number, which ended in three zeros. Three zeroes was very impres-sive. In Manhattan you had to be pretty big to rate even two zeros. She knew of one law firm that had managed to get four zeros—their number was something something something, zero zero zero zero. Their machinations had backfired, how-ever. Whenever anyone got a message from the firm, they assumed that some mistake had been made and ended up forcing their receptionist to check the number. So by the time they got through to return the phone call, they were already in a bad mood.

If Star and Wood had three zeros, they probably had a lot of employees. She'd have to have a game plan to get past the receptionist. As far as she could tell by her Housing Court experience, certain people were assigned to certain buildings, sort of like account executives in advertising agencies. So when the receptionist picked up and answered "Star and Wood" in an unhelpful monotone, Nina told her that she was interested in possibly renting space at 545 Madison. She was immediately put through to someone named Jonathan Katz.

"Jonathan Katz speaking." He sounded young.

"Mr. Katz, I'm interested in a floor that used to be rented by HLS Associates at 545 Madison Avenue. I believe that they've vacated. Is that true?"

"You're not another angry investor, are you?" He sounded young and indiscreet. Nina had hit pay dirt.

"Pardon me?" It was usually the best thing to say in such circumstances.

"It's just that I've gotten so many calls, you wouldn't believe it. 'Where did they go, how can I get my hands on them?' I have a phone number I'm supposed to refer all calls to, but people keep calling me back because all they get is an answering service."

"Actually, I'm not that interested in contacting them. I can do that on my own. What I'm really interested in is seeing a copy of their lease."

"Oh, I couldn't do that." Her luck. All of a sudden Jonathan Katz was becoming discreet. "As a managing agent, I'm not authorized to release any information regarding a lease. You'd have to go directly to the landlord for that."

"And who owns 545?" she asked.

"Maplewood Properties. It's one of the Kantor organizations."

"The Kantor family owns a lot of buildings, don't they?" She didn't want to start over at ground zero.

"I'll tell you what. Call Eric Kantor. I'll give you his number. He's in charge of 545. Tell him I told you to call. He's a nice guy, he might help you out. He's sort of the kid brother over there."

She called right away. Eric Kantor seemed eager to chat. Thank God for kid brothers.

"Oh, yeah, HLS. Of course I remember them," he said. "They spent years trying to squirm out of that lease."

"They did?"

"Uh-huh. First they offered me two hundred grand to

terminate. But I knew I'd have a bitch of a time rerenting the space. Especially at the 1986 rates they were paying. So I turned them down. Then they tried to litigate, claiming some crap about incapacity of the managing partner."

Nina's heart raced a bit. "I don't get it." Keep him going, she told herself.

"There was this provision in the lease that the tenant could terminate upon death of the managing partner."

"I've never heard that one before," she said, trying to sound unexcited.

"It's unusual. But not unheard of. It's used when a company is really a one-man operation, even though it's technically a corporation or partnership. In fact, I saw it again recently in a lease for a lawyer who was a P.C."

"I see." P.C. meant professional corporation. Many lawyers made themselves into P.C.'s, as did doctors and accountants.

"That way," Kantor said, "if the guy died, the estate wouldn't have to dissolve the corporation before they could vacate the space."

"And who was the managing partner of HLS?"

"Mark Hirsch."

"I didn't realize it was a one-person operation. What about Levinson and Silver?"

"Hirsch really was HLS. He was the rainmaker, getting the investors, putting together the deals. Silver was really just a glorified investor and Levinson, as far as I could tell, was more of an office manager."

"You said they sued you. What was the basis of the litigation?"

"There was no basis. It was a bunch of trumped-up horseshit. They said that Hirsch was incapacitated because of some illness I don't even believe that he had. Severe diabetes, they claimed. The guy looked all right to me. Anyway, their claim was that this incapacity was tantamount to death, so they should be let out of the lease."

"And what happened?"

"What do you think happened? My lawyer got it thrown out on a motion for summary judgment. They never had a case. Not even close. Then they came to me with their tails between their legs, offering me three hundred grand to let them out of the lease. But I turned them down again."

"How come? They were probably on the verge of bankruptcy. Wouldn't three hundred thousand dollars have helped to cut your losses?"

"No. My bottom line was seven figures."

"Why?"

"Because I'm not an idiot. Because from the moment these guys came to me I knew they were flimflam men who wouldn't be able to withstand the slightest downturn in the market. And this was in eighty-six, when I could have rented to whoever I wanted. I wasn't going to enter into a long-term lease without some collateral."

"And the collateral was worth a million dollars?"

"Yup."

"What was it?"

"Steve Silver's house."

Nina's first thought was whether or not the Silver residence was worth a million dollars. She was no expert on Great Neck real estate values. Besides, it had been dark when she was there. She couldn't tell how big the backyard was, and whether or not they had a swimming pool or a tennis court.

Nina's second thought was the one that counted. But it was only after she had obsessed about the backyard for a while that it sunk in. Unless Mark Hirsch was killed, Steve Silver was going to lose his home.

She tried to sound calm. "From what I hear," she said,

"you would have been better off with the three hundred thousand."

"Yeah, who knew the guy was going to drive himself off the road? The odds seemed like a million to one. And now I'm stuck with a whole floor of office space that's still vacant."

"Well, you took a calculated risk and lost. Happens all the time. Nothing you can do about it."

"I guess not." Eric Kantor sounded forlorn, like the kid brother wasn't exactly knocking the rest of the family dead with his wild success.

"So HLS stopped paying their rent right after Hirsch died?" she asked.

"Well, that's what was so screwy."

"What was so screwy?"

"According to my managing agent, they hadn't paid December's rent. Almost as if they knew this was going to happen."

"That's pretty interesting, isn't it?" she said. "Who usually paid the rent?"

"The managing agent takes care of all that. The only reason I'm familiar with the details was that collecting HLS's rent had become like pulling teeth. Every month was a major negotiation, so Jonathan was consulting me all the time, asking me if this or that was acceptable."

"HLS must have been pretty tapped out, huh?"

"I'll say. The last couple of months, Steve Silver was writing the rent checks on his personal account. The joint checking account he had with his wife, for God's sake. It was really pathetic."

"And he never sent in December's rent?"

"I didn't say that. Jonathan got a check around the middle of the month, which was common. They were chronically late by that time. He ran to deposit it, of course. But it was too late. Silver's bank had received a stop payment order. And the next thing you know Hirsch was dead and they were off the hook. Makes you wonder, doesn't it?"

It certainly did. Kevin Karp had told Nina that he had located Mark on December 14th. He had called Beverly right away. If Beverly had told Steve Silver where her husband was, there would have been plenty of time for him to cancel the rent check before arranging to have Mark killed.

"It certainly makes me wonder," Nina said. "Mr. Kantor, you have been most helpful. I would like to thank you for your time. If there's anything I can do for you, please let me know."

"Well, if you know anyone who wants to rent the eleventh floor of 545 Madison Avenue, send them my way, will you?"

He sounded a little flirtatious. It briefly occurred to her that she had just spent fifteen minutes on the phone talking to someone who might have been one of the most eligible young bachelors on the island of Manhattan. Yet she had made absolutely no effort to cast her line. She knew women who paid hundreds of dollars to go to a charity event simply because they had heard that an unmarried male Tisch would be present. And here was a Kantor, galloping out of her life.

Too bad. She was finally hot on the trail of Mark Hirsch's killer. If she hesitated now, all might be lost. She had to get to Beverly and find out the truth about whether or not she had revealed her husband's whereabouts to Steve Silver.

Besides, these real estate families weren't worth what they used to be. "Thanks again," she said, and disconnected herself from Eric Kantor and any possibilities he presented.

27

She called Beverly, and Lisa answered. Her mother would be home around six, she said. Nina knew that she should go out there and talk to Beverly in person, but the thought of the Long Island Rail Road made her sick. It was so lame, trying to conduct an investigation using a suburban commuter line. What the hell, it was time for a trip to Brooklyn.

Her sister picked up the phone on the sixth ring. One of the problems with brownstone living was that you had to live your life on four levels.

"Oh, Nina, I was just on my way over to the Gardens." Twice a week, Laura did her Girl Guide routine at the Brooklyn Botanic Gardens. "You're lucky you caught me."

Laura always made the life of a housewife sound like a madcap whirl. Nina was never successful at convincing herself that her sister was trying to cover up for what amounted to just a lot of drudgery. She couldn't banish the sneaking suspicion that as far as housewifery went, the more money you had, the more madcap and the less drudgeful your life could be. And Laura wasn't doing too badly. She had live-in help, a personal trainer, calligraphy classes, and a part-time furniture restoration business for extra meaningfulness.

So much for money not being able to buy happiness. "Boy, that invitation got there fast," Laura said.

"Excuse me?" Nina didn't know what her sister was talking about. But she had a strong premonition that the conversation would leave her once again amazed at how remarkably self-absorbed Laura was.

"Aren't you calling to RSVP about Evan's birthday party?"

"Actually, I'm calling to borrow your car this afternoon." It was hardly Laura's car, since she didn't drive. But those distinctions didn't seem to count anymore.

"Oh, Ken has it. He took it with him today because he had a tennis game this morning over in Queens." Laura's husband had a dermatology practice on Central Park West and a membership in a Long Island City racquet club. And two cars. He kept the Range Rover out in the Hamptons.

"Do you think he'll lend it to me?"

"I don't see why not. Call him."

"Okay."

"So are you coming?" Laura asked.

"Why would I come out to Brooklyn if the car is in Manhattan?"

"Are you coming to Evan's birthday party?"

"When is it?"

"I thought you got the invitation."

"*You* thought I got the invitation. That doesn't mean that I got the invitation."

Nina must have sounded pretty snotty, because Laura got defensive. "Okay, you don't have to make a big deal out of it. But let me know when you do get it, because I'd like to know what you think."

"I'm sure I'll be able to come."

"I mean, what you think about the invitation. I hand-lettered them." She and her sister were talking at cross-purposes again. They had always been facing in different directions, ever since childhood. But they had at least been able to talk to each other over their shoulders from time to time. And they had always had a good time at Loehmann's. But since the birth of her third child, Laura had been hitting new heights of self-absorption.

Nina curbed her annoyance. "I'll call you as soon as I get the invitation. I promise. And I'm sure they're lovely. You hand-letter so well." It was true. Nina's calligraphy, on the other hand, looked like it was done by someone with an advanced case of Parkinson's.

"Thank you," her sister said. "I do find it calming. Whenever I'm getting really stressed out—"

Nina cut her off. "Could you give me Ken's office number? I'm sort of in a big hurry."

"All right." Laura gave her the number. Her brother-in-law was a big man. His phone number ended in two zeroes.

"Thanks. Maybe I'll see you tonight when I drop off the car."

"Do you think you'll stay for dinner? Because I was thinking of grilling salmon steaks." Laura's kitchen had a Jenn-Air stove that featured indoor grilling with downdraft ventilation, as she had explained a multitude of times. "But I only have two and if you're going to be here maybe I'll stop on my way back and get—"

"No." Nina cut her off again. Once Laura got started, she could run through the entire contents of all three Silver Palate cookbooks. "I'm sure I won't be there before nine."

"What do you need the car for?"

Nina was starting to feel the inadequacy one feels while sustaining a phone conversation with someone who has gotten everything they ever wanted out of life. If she was going to keep up her momentum and confront Beverly, she'd better get off the phone right away. "It's an emergency," Nina said. "I'll tell you about it when I see you."

"Okay, don't forget about the invitation."

"I won't." Nina rolled her eyes, hung up, and called Ken. He was, of course, with a patient. "Tell him it's Nina and I need to borrow his car," she said to his secretary.

"Okay." The secretary returned to the phone after a few moments. "He gave me the keys," she said. "You can pick them up here anytime until five-thirty. The car's in a garage on Amsterdam near Seventy-fifth."

"Thanks. I'll be over by five." That was the good thing about having an emotionally withholding doctor for a brother-in-law. Unlike his wife, he was too busy to get on the phone and make you feel inadequate.

But she felt inadequate anyway, just walking into his office. Being there always made her question the validity of her existence. Not that it took much. But this was worse. Everything seemed so controlled, so orderly, to make so much sense. Kenneth Rubin, father of three, curer of disease, master of racquet sports.

He had well-scrubbed, neatly trimmed nails and his skin gave off an affluent glow. Maybe it was the weekend salt air out in the Hamptons, maybe it was all that post-tennis blood rushing around in his capillaries, or maybe it was the expensive *schmearochs* he rubbed in daily from the tiny tubes he received as free samples. Whatever it was, her brother-in-law had the skin of a man whose life was going the way he wanted.

Ken had been too busy to get on the phone and he was too busy to pop his head out when Nina picked up the car keys. It was just as well. It was easier for her to maintain her woman-warrior stance without having him give her pores a quick once-over while kissing her hello.

The secretary gave her the garage stub along with the keys. Nina told her to tell Ken that she would drop the car off at his house later on that evening. When she got to the garage, she had to double back to the cash machine on Seventy-second to retrieve enough money to get the car out. Ken spent as much on monthly parking as Nina did on rent.

She hated driving her brother-in-law's car. It made her nervous. Not that it was awfully expensive or anything, only a Honda Prelude. But it was as well-scrubbed and groomed as Ken's fingernails. And sliding behind the wheel of it never made her feel as though she was going to have a triumphant adventure, the way she had felt in the rental car. Instead, she felt like someone might open their car door too close by and she'd return Ken's car with a new ding. Which wasn't exactly her idea of an exciting adventure.

She drove up Amsterdam and turned east on Eighty-first Street. Going east on West Eighty-first was always an unusual surprise, since odd-numbered streets in Manhattan went west. Except that they had redirected Eighty-first so that you could cut through Central Park without detouring. The downside was that even though you entered the park on Eighty-first, you came out on Seventy-ninth. Which meant you lost two blocks if you were heading uptown. Which Nina was, of course.

28 . . . .

Beverly was already home by the time Nina arrived, after bumbling around Manhasset Hills, making a couple of wrong turns. She had been confused by the split-levelness of it all. Besides, the eastbound traffic out of the city at five o'clock had been murder. The Grand Central Parkway during rush hour made the IRT seem like a magic carpet—even with the globules of spit and an occasional rat on the tracks.

Luckily there was no gray Mercedes in the driveway. She'd try to talk fast, since Nina had a strong feeling that Stuart Grossman's arrival would put a damper on the conversation.

"Hello there," she said in a show-businessy voice, when Beverly opened the door. "Thought I'd drop in for a chat. It's been a while."

Beverly was wearing her ubiquitous black spandex leggings, topped with an oversize sweatshirt. The shirt was from the schmuckosaurus line, matching her coffee mugs. This one featured a dinosaur weighed down by child paraphernalia, captioned Momasaurus. Nina found it more annoying than cute, but it gave her an idea for an angle.

"Come in, I guess," Beverly said unenthusiastically. She stepped aside. Nina noticed that she was barefoot. Barefoot was better than high heels. It minimized their height disparity, making Nina feel more powerful. "I think we should go into the den."

"Fine." They stepped down the three stairs to the den, where Lisa was sprawled on the couch with Bunny. The television blared. "Hi, Lisa," Nina said. "How are you?"

"Okay." The kid was watching her like a hawk.

Beverly turned off the TV.

"I've got to talk to your mother for a little while."

"Okay." Lisa made no move off the couch.

"Alone." Nina tried to sound bossy. Lisa still didn't move.

"Upstairs." Beverly sounded bossy effortlessly. Lisa left the room.

Perhaps there was a God, and he or she had not seen fit to allow Nina to reproduce, since she was obviously incapable of disciplining another human being. But if she couldn't get a teenager to move her ass, how was she going to get Beverly to spill her guts?

"Now, Beverly," Nina began, upping her attempt to sound firm, "I have a few questions for you. And they're important ones. I would appreciate it if you didn't evade them or try to bullshit me. Because even if you don't care whether or not anyone gets to the bottom of your husband's death, I think you owe it to your daughter to find out the truth. You know that Lisa is suffering, don't you?"

Beverly's lower lip trembled, but she didn't say anything.

"She's making herself throw up. You did know that, didn't you?"

"Lisa's been throwing up for a long time. Since before her father died."

"And you've just been ignoring it?"

Now Beverly did start to cry. "Of course not. Do you think I'm some kind of a monster? She's been seeing a therapist for years. Poor kid, she's had a lot to deal with." Beverly started to sob in a big way, tears streaming, nose running, and shoulders shaking.

Nina rummaged around in her purse and found a tissue that met minimum sanitary standards of acceptability. She handed it to Beverly.

"Look," Nina said, "don't you think it's time to come clean? About everything? Especially about why everyone kept their mouth shut when they knew that there was no way Mark could have been killed in a drunk-driving accident."

Beverly let out a sob-choked sigh. "I don't know who killed Mark. Honestly I don't. All I can tell you is what I do know."

"That's all I'm asking."

"The first thing you should understand is that Mark and I were both having affairs. I'm sure Lisa must have known. She knows everything."

"I've noticed."

"Maybe that's why she has that problem. Who knows? Anyway, Mark had been sleeping with his secretary for a long time."

"Donna?"

"Uh-huh."

"She told me she was in love with him," Nina said, "but she claims that they never had sex."

Beverly shrugged. "That's not true. She was always trying to stop, afraid her fiancé would find out. But then she would break down and jump back into bed with him."

"How do you know all this?"

"Jerry Levinson told me. We're very close."

"Is that who you were having the affair with?"

"Of course not." Beverly sounded offended. "You don't think I'm the kind of person who would sleep with my husband's business partner, do you?"

"Who were you sleeping with? If I may ask."

"Stuart, of course. I'm also not the kind of person who jumps from one bed to another. Stuart was the first and only." Beverly got a funny look on her face.

"Except for?" Nina prompted.

"Except for a masseur down in Palm-Aire. Once. Years ago." The admission was promising. Beverly was in a mood to come clean. "Stuart and I just had a lot of chemistry. He was one of Mark's investors and would come by the house from time to time. He was still married, but barely. His wife had retreated into her own world, which did not include him."

Nina started to feel as if she were watching a movie. People did not talk like this on the West Side. At least not the people she knew, who were preoccupied with chiropractors and couples therapists.

"He came on very strong," Beverly said. "From the moment we met. He'd call me all the time, telling me how sexy I was and all. And he'd come by during the day when Mark wasn't here, following me around the house, whispering and sticking his tongue in my ear."

The old tongue in the ear, Nina thought. Who could resist that? "I see."

"And I guess I wasn't feeling so good about myself since Jerry told me about Mark and Donna. I was starved for appreciation. And Mark had become more and more obsessed with the business, which was falling apart. So I finally said yes to Stuart."

Nina felt somewhat sympathetic. She had done the same once or twice.

"When Mark disappeared, I was furious. Even though I knew that our marriage had its problems, I couldn't believe he would run out on Lisa that way. So I hired someone to find him. Although between the time I hired Karp and the time he found Mark, Stuart had left his wife. Which kind of changed the picture."

Nina must have looked a little sour, because Beverly started to cry again. "I'll bet you think that I'm a horrible gold-digging slut. And believe me, I feel guilty about plenty of things. Don't you think that every time I hear Lisa in the bathroom I feel like shit? But I think that Stuart genuinely loves me. And he was being so generous toward me and Lisa, that when Karp phoned to tell me he had found Mark in Lake Placid, I couldn't decide what to do. I mean, in some way I was so happy after he left. It was such a relief. After I found out where he was, I just sat and obsessed and did nothing and the next thing I knew, Mark was dead."

"And no one said anything about the fact that he was supposedly drunk?"

"Not at first."

"Did his mother know?"

"I never told Helen. But after a while Jerry and I discussed it, so the whole office must have known."

"And no one called the police or anything?"

"Jerry said I looked as relieved as Donna, who was now going ahead and planning her wedding. And Steve and Jerry were relieved, too, because now they could get out of their lease. You see, there was this clause that—"

"I know all about it."

"Oh." Beverly looked confused. Nina decided to take advantage of the moment.

"Beverly," she said sharply, "your daughter thinks that

you might be responsible for her father's death. It's very important that you don't lie to me. Did you tell anyone that Mark was in Lake Placid before he died?"

"No, I swear I didn't. Not Lisa, not Helen, not even Stuart."

"Did you know that Steve Silver had pledged his house as collateral for the lease?"

"No. But Steve wouldn't have killed Mark. Not for something like that. They were best friends. Steve loved to hang around Mark. He misses him terribly."

"Kevin Karp told me that you were referred to him by one of Mark's business associates. Did Karp know Steve Silver? Could he have told him where Mark was without your knowledge?"

"No way," Beverly said. "They hated each other."

"What do you mean?"

"They knew each other all right. But Steve's not the one who referred me to Kevin Karp. Karp's been trailing Steve for a long time, finding him in all sorts of compromising positions with all kinds of women. For Kathy's divorce. Her alleged divorce. Which I'm damn sure she'll never do anything about."

"Kathy?"

"Steve's wife. Who's been talking about divorcing him for years. She's the one who gave me Karp's phone number. Kathy Silver."

"I always hated that woman," Lisa called from the top of the stairs.

29 . . . .

"**For Chrissakes, Lisa,**" Beverly yelled. "**Can't you ever** mind your own business? Even for a minute?"

Lisa came running down the stairs. "She did it. I know she did it. It's Kathy's fault that Daddy died."

"You really think so?" Nina asked.

"Not that she did it herself, of course," Lisa said. "She must have hired someone to do it. The way she hires someone to do everything. Her garden, her hair, her dog, everything."

"Lisa, watch what you say," Beverly warned.

"But Mommy, you said yourself that she probably hires someone to wipe her ass, didn't you?"

"Look," Nina cut in, "let's stipulate that Kathy is a heavy user of consumer services. But a contract killer . . ."

"I don't know," Beverly said. "I'm not sure I can picture it. Making an appointment to have your legs waxed is one thing. Making an appointment to have your husband's business partner murdered is another."

"Why is it so hard to picture?" Lisa asked. "She probably put it on her charge card."

Nina wasn't sure she could picture it either. She went over the dates in her head. The following scenario was possible: on December 14th, Karp finds Mark in Lake Placid and calls Kathy even before he calls Beverly. On December 15th, Kathy runs out and hires someone to push Mark over a cliff. By December 20th, he's dead. It sounded farfetched.

December 15th. It reminded Nina of something. Eric Kantor had told her that they received December's rent on the 15th, but by the time they tried to cash it, someone had stopped payment on the check. Which reminded her of something else Kantor had said. That the check was written on the joint account that Silver had with his wife. So Kathy could have stopped payment, knowing Mark was soon to be dead. It was definitely suspicious.

Nina had caught a glimpse of Kathy Silver, but all she could remember was a southwestern apron and a matte gold *chai*. Both fashion accessories were a little off, but not necessarily indicative of sociopathy. Or were they?

She tried again. "What do you think?" she asked Beverly. "Within the realm of possibility?"

"I don't know," Beverly said.

"I'll put money on it," Lisa said.

"Keep in mind that Steve had pledged his house as collateral for the lease, and that he stood in great danger of losing it," Nina reminded Beverly.

"Her home was very important to her. You know who we should talk to?"

"Who?"

"Elaine Levinson. Jerry's wife. She's known Kathy for years."

"Can we trust her?"

"Absolutely. She hates Kathy."

"That isn't what I meant," Nina said. "Can we trust her judgment? I mean, if she hates Kathy, that might cloud her analytic abilities."

"I don't care about her analytic abilities," Beverly said. "I just want to know if she's heard anything. She lives a couple of blocks away. I'll give her a call and tell her to come over." She checked her watch. "If she's not in the middle of making dinner. Even though both of her kids are away at school, she still cooks." Beverly pronounced the word "cooks" with distaste, the way a nun might say "fucks."

Elaine Levinson did turn out to be in the middle of making dinner. But luckily whatever she was cooking was on autoroast in the microwave, so she came right over.

The first thought that Nina had when Elaine walked through the door was "Thank God, a normal person." Elaine was fiftyish, chubbyish, and graying. She wore simple wool slacks and a pullover that was devoid of slogans and decoration. Her shoes were flat loafers and her jewelry was the kind that used to be enough—a gold wedding band, pearl earrings, and a Seiko. Her hair was closely cropped. Nina couldn't help feeling that anyone who still had small hair and a Seiko in this town could be trusted.

"Nice to meet you," Elaine said, with the kind of dignified borough accent that Nina was used to. It was definitely there, but not strong enough to distract. She shook Nina's hand calmly and firmly.

Beverly launched into a somewhat scattered version of the facts. Elaine listened without interrupting and nodded thoughtfully from time to time. "What do you think?" Lisa asked impatiently, when Beverly finally got to the part about Steve using his house as collateral.

"Well, you know . . ." Elaine hesitated.

"What?"

"I always thought that Kathy was having an affair with Kevin Karp."

"You're kidding," Beverly said.

My God, these middle-aged people in the suburbs screwed like bunnies. That was the problem with getting married while you were young. If you waited until you were forty, like all those people in the city, you were so busy at the fertility doctor that you didn't have time to have affairs.

"You know how Steve was," Elaine said to Beverly. She turned to Nina. "A real panty-sniffer. Kathy always talked about divorcing him, and Karp had been having someone tail him for years. They were always finding him in hotels and on boats with young blondes. But Kathy never filed for divorce. And I think part of the reason was that she was hooked on Kevin Karp. She couldn't bear to end their business relationship, for fear that their personal relationship would end too."

"Part of the reason," Lisa repeated. "But not all. Don't forget about Steve's money. And the house and the boat and all the racehorses."

"Should she be listening to this?" Elaine asked Beverly.

"She listens to everything," Beverly said. "There doesn't seem to be anything I can do about it."

"It's actually Steve's father's money," Lisa continued. "So if Kathy got divorced, she probably couldn't get her greedy hands on any of it. Or not enough to count, anyway."

"The money is very important to Kathy," Elaine agreed. "She grew up in a small town. Dead father, mother a waitress in a truck stop, that sort of thing. But she's far from stupid. An aunt sent her to Ohio State and that's where she met Steve. As soon as they started dating, she hung on for dear life."

"How long have you known her?" Nina asked Elaine.

"At least twenty years. Jerry worked for Steve's father even before Kathy and Steve got married. I remember when

Steve brought her back East. His parents had a conniption, of course. She looked like a real small-town girl, but very beautiful. And before you knew it, she was Japping it up with the best of them. Hair, clothes, jewelry . . . God, she was a quick study."

"Did Steve's parents eventually come around?"

"When she converted to Judaism, I think they realized that there was no way out of it."

Religious conversion was so strange to Nina. How could you make yourself into something you weren't? Not that she was against it. She knew some people who had converted for beautiful and spiritual reasons. About 2 percent. She had a very strong suspicion that the motivation for the other 98 percent was directly proportional to the financial status of their intended. And there was an undeniable sexism. It was the women who always got talked into it. Men who converted were as rare as men with nose jobs, another thing women got talked into much too often.

"So once she converted," Nina asked, "they started to accept her?"

"They let up once the grandchildren were born. And his father eventually got quite fond of Kathy. But he still keeps a close watch on the money. As I said, she was a quick study and she remains a habituée of Bulgari."

"Is that where she got that weird *chai* she was wearing?" Nina asked.

"I think she had that custom made."

"So it isn't as if Steve's parents are really starving her, is it?"

"No, but they are much more generous with her kids than with her. It's obvious."

"And if Steve had to sell the house to pay off the rest of the lease, what would have happened?"

"Hard to say. I'm sure Herb, Steve's father, never knew

that it was pledged. He would never have allowed it. Herb Silver wasn't too hot on the idea of HLS to begin with. He couldn't understand why Steve didn't want to stick around in the family business and reap all the rewards that Herb had spent a lifetime sowing."

"So Steve's father would have let them swing in the wind?" Nina asked.

"He would have bailed him out to an extent, I guess. Neither Herb nor Ruth, his wife, would have wanted to see their grandchildren deprived. But I don't think he'd run out and buy them another house in Kings Point. Steve and Kathy would definitely have to downscale. And live life listening to Herb say 'I told you so' all the time."

"It's so amazing," Nina said. "This all came out because I casually asked my mother if Mark Hirsch had a drinking problem."

"What do you mean?" asked Elaine.

"I noticed on the accident report that Mark was drunk at the time of his death. So, yenta that I am, I asked my mother, who was a friend of Mark's mother, whether he made a habit of hitting the bottle. And she told me that he was a severe diabetic who couldn't drink."

"I didn't know that," Elaine said.

"You didn't?" asked Beverly. "Jerry knew. He never told you?"

"Nope."

"Did Kathy know?" Nina asked Beverly.

"I don't know."

"Kathy never mentioned it to me," Elaine said. "As a matter of fact, I bet she didn't know. Because I remember her planning a dinner party and she was trying to figure out how many bottles of wine to buy. And she said to me that Mark didn't drink much, did he? And I said I didn't think so. But

I'm sure she used the word 'much.' She certainly didn't say that he didn't drink at all."

"There you go," said Lisa. "She made a phone call, probably to one of those guys that Steve hangs around with at the track. And told him she'd give him her diamond ring if he'd get my father drunk and push his car over a cliff. And because she didn't know that he didn't drink, she didn't know that anyone would get suspicious about it."

It sounded much less farfetched now. Nina felt she should take action, rush out and immediately do something. But she didn't know exactly what to do. And instead here she was, starring in her seventeen millionth episode of *A Coupla White Chicks Sitting Around Talking*.

30 · · · · · ·

A tricky business, this shiksaphobia. It was very possible that Kathy Silver had arranged Mark's death. On the other hand, when you had four Jewish women in a room discussing a thin, blond Gentile woman who had married a rich Jewish man, it was easy to get carried away.

Nina tried hard not to indulge. She herself had all sorts of friends—Christians who had married Jews, Jews who had married Christians, Christians who had married Christians, and even a few Jews who had married Jews. She held no prejudices. As far as she was concerned, if you could actually find someone to marry and then make it work, you could play by whatever rules you chose to write.

But there was no point in pretending that she never thought about the fact that the acquisition of a non-Jewish wife was becoming a mandatory status symbol in this country. Magazines ran articles about these trophy wives; novelists and filmmakers used them liberally as stock characters. The worst was television. Every time you turned on the tube, there they were—sensitive, attractive, successful, dark-haired Jewish male characters; lawyers and doctors and advertising executives. All created in the image of the television writers and producers who thought them up. And all married to gracious, understanding Christian women with whom they had terrific sexual chemistry.

Intermarriage had run rampant on network television back in the eighties, and showed no sign of abating. There had been the Steadmans of *thirtysomething* and the Markowitzes of *L.A. Law*. The all-time record had been set by Helen Rosenthal of *St. Elsewhere*, a blond Brit who had married five Jewish men. And now there was *Brooklyn Bridge*, with a male Jewish protagonist who was already dating a shiksa even though he was only fourteen. Nina had read somewhere that the only television family who reflected traditional Jewish values were the Huxtables of *The Cosby Show*. And they, of course, were black.

There were a few Jewish female characters knocking around television, none of them married, not even dating. Mostly mothers and sisters and cousins. The Catholics might be burdened by the whore/Madonna syndrome, but at least they had their whores. Jews seemed to be mired in this mother/sister syndrome. Of course, the men who put these shows on the air would tell you that this is what the public wanted to see. That the year they married Rhoda off, the show's ratings plummeted. That certainly offered no comfort.

Nina had always had a difficult history with Jewish men. For a while she considered handing out cards that said "My name is Nina Fischman. At some point I will remind you of your mother. Your mission, should you accept it, is to get past that." So far it had remained mission impossible.

It certainly looked like Kathy might have knocked Mark off. Nina was willing to buy it. But she wanted to make sure she hadn't gotten caught up in let's-blame-the-shiksa-wife fever. The person to talk to was Steve Silver, but she didn't know if she could summon the nerve. Besides, why should he rat on his wife?

On the other hand, why shouldn't he? The Silvers' marriage had to qualify as one of the all-time worst. Hadn't Kathy hired a private detective who had been following him for years? Maybe Steve had been desperately waiting all this time for Kathy to be hauled off to jail, freeing him to spend the rest of his life bimbo-hopping. Nina doubted it, though. Chronic cheaters like him never wanted to get divorced.

She'd have to think of a better angle, some way that she could drive a wedge between husband and wife. For starters, she had to figure out what a man like Steve Silver would be most interested in. That was an easy one. Himself. And if Nina told him that he was the prime suspect in the murder of Mark Hirsch, he might come clean to save his own hide.

Elaine gave her directions to the Silvers' house. The directions were clear, but Nina had trouble finding it anyway. Being a New Yorker, Nina basically knew from north and south and east and west. Manhattan was a beautiful grid that worked by longitude and latitude. You never went in or out, you always went up or down. She had the general idea that the Silvers lived farther north. And, as she remembered from her conversation with the Israeli cabdriver, in Great Neck north was better. Driving up Middle Neck Road was easy, but once she got into Kings Point and all its curves, she lost her way.

She finally found his block, cut her lights, and drove past his house. There was only one car in the driveway, with a license plate that said KATH4. Thank God for vanity plates. You could tell who was home without peering into the window. Steve apparently was not back yet. Luckily, the Silvers' house was on a dead-end street, so she didn't have to decide which direction he'd be coming from. She turned around, parked at the corner, turned on the radio, and waited.

His was the first car to pass by, a BMW that she recognized from her last visit. She honked and he pulled over. He turned off his ignition and they both lowered their windows. "Oh, it's you," he said, annoyed. "What do you want?"

"I want to talk to you."

"I've got to get home. I'm late."

"It's important."

"Nice car," he said.

She refrained from explaining about her brother-in-law the doctor. If a mint condition Honda Prelude was going to soften this guy up, that was fine with her. "Want to see it from the inside?" she asked.

"Thanks, I'll pass." But he did sound a bit warmer.

"Well, can I get into your car then? It's freezing with the windows down."

"Why don't we go into my house?"

"I don't think that's a good idea. I've really got to talk to you in private."

"About what?" he asked.

"About Mark Hirsch. As you know, I've been trying to get to the bottom of his death, which appears to have been a murder. Mostly for the sake of his daughter. She's been quite shaken by the whole thing."

"Poor Lisa. She's always had a hard time. I'm sure this hasn't helped."

"No, it hasn't. But one thing that would help would be finding out how her father died. You know, she went through a stage of blaming her mother."

"Beverly?" Steve grinned. "I'm sure there were plenty of times when Beverly felt like killing Mark. But there's no way she would have really done it."

"I agree. And the facts seem to bear that out. Actually, everything seems to point to you."

Steve smirked. "All right, I can see it's time to confess. After all, you've got me here all alone, on a dark, deserted street."

Nina found it incredible that he managed to be condescending, considering the circumstances. Maybe she should think about carrying a gun. But a gun probably wouldn't be a very fitting extension of her self-image. "Why don't you just tell me what happened?" She tried to affect that monotone that Mel had mastered up in Lake Placid. But her voice shook. She was no Mel.

"I don't really know what happened." A noticeable whine had crept into his voice. He reached over abruptly and turned off his lights with resentment, the way an eight-year-old boy would throw down his baseball glove when he was called home to dinner. He raised his window, got out, and walked over to the Honda. He opened the door on the passenger side and slid in beside her.

She thought about locking him in with the automatic door-lock mechanism for effect, but she wasn't sure about how to use it. And fumbling around with it certainly wouldn't help intimidate him. She really didn't know how to get to Steve. So far he didn't seem too worried. There was a smugness about him that she couldn't seem to penetrate. He was still perfectly groomed, wearing an even more expensive sweater than last time.

She decided to plunge right in. "Listen, maybe you want to pretend that this is all a big joke, but it's not. I've already spoken to the police in Lake Placid, and they're conducting a continuing investigation. And I have a piece of information that I'm sure they'd be interested in."

"Oh, yeah? What's that?"

"That HLS's ten-year lease on office space, which you

were trying so hard to break, had your house pledged as collateral. And that only the death of the managing partner could get you out of it."

"Very interesting." He hadn't even twitched. "Can I go home now? I'm missing *Wheel of Fortune*."

She felt like smacking him. "And that if Mark hadn't died, you would have lost your home. And I'm sure your wife wouldn't have been too pleased about that. In fact," said Nina, using another approach, trying to bring Kathy into it, "your wife probably didn't even know it was pledged. Whose name is the house in, by the way?"

"None of your business." Steve Silver was becoming more like an eight-year-old by the minute.

"Do you and Kathy have joint title?"

"As a matter of fact, it's not in my name at all," he said, with elementary school sarcasm. "So there goes my motive for killing Mark."

"So it's in Kathy's name?"

"Nope."

"Who owns it?"

"I'm going home now."

She put her hand on his shoulder and turned him around to face her. "Look," she said firmly, as if she were teaching a third-grade class, "it's easy for me to find out whose name your house is in. I can do a title search, which will take less than an hour. So you might as well tell me now."

"Are you Jewish?" This time his sarcasm sounded a little more grown-up.

"Is the Pope Catholic?"

"You don't know much about the way that Jewish families work, do you?"

"Not Jewish families with money."

"You're not playing dumb with me, are you?"

"I never play dumb. Women like me can't afford to."

"Well, let me educate you. Jewish parents don't part with their assets until they're dead. Then you get the whole enchilada at once. There's no word for trust fund in Yiddish."

Now she got it. The guy who owned the Mercedes-Benz and the fancy leather jacket also owned the house his son lived in.

"I see. And your father was willing to pledge the house as collateral for your office lease?"

"Not quite." Nina might have been imagining it, but suddenly Steve sounded like he was on the verge of tears. His voice was croaky and his lip was trembling. So that was his Achilles' heel. Daddy.

"He didn't know about the pledge, did he?"

"No."

"Did you forge his signature?"

"Maybe."

"And he found out?"

"Maybe."

"How?"

"How do you think?"

"Kathy?"

"How else would he find out?"

It made more sense now. Kathy didn't have to hire someone to have Mark killed. All she had to do was call her father-in-law. "So your father was responsible for killing Mark?"

Steve swallowed hard. Some of his composure returned. "I don't really know what happened. I'm telling you the honest truth. My father and I hardly speak anymore, ever since I left his business to start up HLS. But he can be a real cocksucking bastard, I'll tell you that. You should talk to Kathy about it. She always knows what's going on with him. She and my father are powerful allies."

"Allies? I'm surprised." Now Nina was playing dumb. She hadn't forgotten the big hug and kiss that Herb had given Kathy at her front door. "I thought your father had trouble accepting your marriage to Kathy."

"Sure he had trouble. So did my mother. But you know how Jewish parents are. They eat your guts out about marrying the wrong woman, but they'll gang up with her against you whenever it suits their purposes. Anyway, both my father and Kathy hated Mark. They hated the whole idea of HLS. Neither of them could understand why I would want to leave the family business; I had such a good thing going. They thought Mark was some kind of Svengali who had me under his spell."

"Did he?"

"He was an exciting guy, doing exciting things."

For a brief moment, Nina wondered whether Steve's pursuit of such a long string of young blondes was simply a sublimation of latent homosexuality. Maybe he *was* in love with Mark. It was an intriguing possibility, but she put it out of her mind. She'd think about it later. Why muddle things now, when she was finally getting somewhere. "Everyone seems to be in agreement about Mark's charisma. I hadn't seen him in about twenty years, so I really couldn't say. But I do remember having an intense crush on him when I was eight."

"Right. Well, he never changed. He was a superb pitch man, could get anybody to invest in anything. And he had some really creative ideas. It wasn't his fault the whole thing went bust. You can't do much in a market like this. But I believed in him."

"Which is why you put yourself on the line like that? Forging your father's signature and all."

"Yeah. Pledging the house as collateral was the only way we could get such favorable terms on the lease. And I never thought we'd have to bail out. No one knew about it except

Mark and Jerry. Not even Kathy. She would have killed me. And she didn't find out until last November."

"How did she find out?"

"Well, I was forced to write the October rent check out of my personal account. HLS was just tapped out. There was nothing else to do."

"And Kathy saw the canceled check when it came back from the bank the following month?"

"Right. And was she pissed. Said I was throwing good money after bad; why didn't I just walk away from HLS and go back into my father's business. I was lucky I still had options, all that stuff. That's when I told her that the house was pledged. And that my father didn't know about it. She went apeshit."

"I'll bet. And did you also tell her that if Mark died, you could get out of the lease?"

"No, she found out on her own."

"How do you know?"

"Mark came into the office really shaken one day. It was the middle of November. He had come very close to having a car accident. The night before, I had noticed that someone had been riffling through my file cabinet at home. A copy of the lease was sticking up. I got worried then. I figured she had found out. But I also knew that Kathy could never have managed to fake a car accident. She must have called my father and told him to take care of things."

"Your father sounds like quite a guy."

"He's scary." Steve looked eight years old again. "That's part of why I ran away from the business. He's always had all sorts of goons hanging around there. Anyway, that's when Jerry and I told Mark he might want to get out of town for a while."

"And how did your father find him in Lake Placid?"

"I don't know." Nina couldn't tell if Steve really knew or

not. Perhaps he just wasn't in the mood to have a conversation about Kevin Karp at the moment.

"Did you confront Kathy about this?"

"No."

"Did you confront your father? Try to stop him or anything?"

"No." Steve looked consumed by shame. This sounded like a situation beyond family therapy. "The next thing I knew, he was dead. At first I told myself that it might really have been an accident, since I had no reason to think that anyone had tracked him down. But then Jerry told me about the drunk-driving bit, and I knew that the whole thing had been faked."

"But you decided not to do anything about it?"

"What was I going to do? I mean, I'm not that crazy about my old man, but I didn't want to see him arrested."

"Besides," said Nina, "you were pretty glad to get out of that lease, out of the whole business, weren't you?"

"In a way. You know, my father's dying."

"Really?" So that explained why Steve was being so forthcoming. His father's reign of terror was coming to an end.

"Yup. They opened him up for routine prostate surgery and closed him right back up again. The cancer's reached his liver. He'll be gone soon."

"You sound relieved." Maybe Steve didn't want to see Herb Silver arrested, but wouldn't mind seeing him dead.

He just shrugged. Poor guy. Fathers like Herb Silver were tough. Herb seemed like the kind whose idea of a bar mitzvah present was cutting off their kid's balls and having them gold-plated. And Kathy had played right into her father-in-law's arms, undoubtedly making her husband feel even more inadequate.

Maybe Steve wasn't such an awful character after all. He

had his own issues to deal with. But it was hard for Nina to feel sympathy for the problems of the overprivileged. As Murphy Brown said to Frank, when he signed up for an Iron John workshop, "What's the matter, can't deal with higher pay for equal work?"

31 . . . .

Nina and Steve sat silently in the car for a while, staring out of their respective side windows. Finally, Steve broke the silence. "I'd better be getting home."

"Okay. See you later." The inappropriateness of her response thundered in her ears. Under what circumstances would she be seeing him later? In the D.A.'s office? On the stand in a courtroom? She certainly wouldn't casually run into him at a cocktail party at his tennis club. But "see you later" was a popular method of extricating oneself from social situations, and Nina had used it without thinking.

Steve just nodded and got out of the car. He even waved a little as he got into his.

Nina somehow found her way to the Long Island Expressway, played a hunch on the Interboro Parkway, and then managed to get herself onto the correct side of Prospect Park. For there could be little doubt that her sister lived on the correct side of Prospect Park.

Not that Park Slope was exactly Park Avenue. But it had

come a long way since the days when diminutive Italian widows with black kerchiefs sat perched on brownstone stoops. The local gentry played up the fact that they lived in a borough and wasn't that funky. But the truth was that Park Slope was a place where people paid much closer attention to their kids' ERB and SAT scores than they ever had to the NBA standings. If you were looking for the kind of neighborhood where people drank domestic beer and shot hoops in the schoolyard, you were in the wrong place. No matter how much of a soulful dance anyone did when they told you they lived in Brooklyn.

Nina spent a longer time looking for a parking space than she had talking to Steve Silver. She found one on Third Street, an especially prosperous-looking block with double width sidewalks and a boulevard of trees. She walked the few blocks to Laura's. The Rubins lived in the named rather than the numbered streets, which used to hold cachet. Now that the whole neighborhood had gentrified, it barely mattered.

When Nina rang the bell, Ida answered the door. "Fancy meeting you here," Nina said.

"I'm baby-sitting," her mother explained. "Laura and Ken went to the movies. I just put the kids to bed."

Nina pulled off her coat and threw it on the couch. She sat down beside it. "What are they seeing?" she asked.

"Dances with Wolves."

"My God, they'll be out all night. That isn't the kind of thing you see on a week night. It's a marathon, not a movie."

"I haven't seen it yet," said Ida. "Did you like it?"

"It was touching, in a sort of trite and boring way." Nina thought about it. "Like life," she added.

"What do you think of Kevin Costner?"

"I like Jerry Seinfeld better."

"I don't know if I'd compare the two."

"Costner narrates the film," Nina said, "and I swear, he

sounds like he's in junior high school. He gets away with it, I guess because everyone thinks he's so cute."

"He was certainly cute in *Bull Durham*."

"That movie was calculated to appeal to you. I read somewhere about how mostly older women liked that movie, so I tested the premise. I asked a teenager I knew what she thought about it. She thought it was so-so, but she told me that her mother had seen it eight times."

"Well, if it was calculated to appeal to me, it worked," said Ida.

"I actually paid to see that movie twice," Nina admitted.

"Want something to eat?"

"Okay." They headed downstairs to the kitchen. Nina opened the refrigerator and saw some of those little white cartons that always made her heart thump. She had sworn off Chinese food until Tom's visit, but her vow had not included acts of God. And innocently opening someone else's refrigerator and finding Chinese leftovers definitely counted as an act of God.

She opened a carton cautiously. Cold noodles with sesame sauce—the lifeblood of her generation. It was an omen. She found a fork and dug in. Straight from the carton, of course.

She sat down at the kitchen table. Ida joined her. It was time to turn the conversation around from Kevin Costner to Steve Silver. "Guess what? It wasn't Steve, after all," Nina said.

"That's the guy with no socks, right?"

"Right."

"Who says it wasn't him?"

"He says."

"Well, that certainly nails it down."

"No, really. I believe him. Even though he doesn't wear socks. I just came from seeing him."

"Was he wearing socks?"

"I believe he was. But I can't be sure. It was dark."

"And what were you doing with Steve Silver in the dark, may I ask?"

Nina told her a bit about Steve and Herb and Kathy and their complicated triangular relationship.

"It figures that the father was involved," Ida said. "You shouldn't trust anyone named Silver."

"Why not?"

"Because they've obviously dropped the stein or baum or berg or whatever in an attempt to assimilate. If you're going to change your name, why not go all the way to Smythe or Carruthers or something?"

"How can you be sure that it was a half-assed attempt to assimilate? Maybe he was named Silver to begin with."

"I'm telling you," Ida said, "somewhere along the line something was dropped. All those names—Greenbaum and Silverberg and Rosenfeld—they might sound mundane to you, but think about it. They were chosen carefully, back when Jews were just known as Isaac the peddler and Moishe the tailor. Some Holy Roman Emperor in the fifteenth century told them they had to get last names, so they chose the most lyrical and descriptive ones. Greenbaum means 'green tree.' Silverberg means 'silver mountain.' Rosenfeld means 'field of roses.'"

"An adjective and a noun. Like Native Americans."

"Right. So cutting the name in half . . . well, it's like being named Running Bear and dropping the Bear. Why go through life being named Running?"

There was a punchline somewhere in all this that ended with Running Nose, but Nina couldn't come up with it. "Very interesting," she said. "But what do I do now?"

"There are two things you could do. The first and simplest is that you could call the police upstate and tell them everything that Steve Silver told you. And that would be enough. It's not up to you to determine whether or not he's telling the truth. You could just make the phone call and forget about the whole thing. But be careful."

"Of what?"

"I've been worried ever since somebody threw that crate at you in the subway."

"Oh, please. I told you that had nothing to do with this. Do you honestly think that Herb and Kathy Silver dug up a subway grating to drop a crate on my head? No way. It would ruin her manicure."

"So it was just one of those things?"

"Just one of those New York things," Nina sang back.

"This town might be getting too much for me," Ida said.

"Bullshit. Don't you start New York–bashing. If *you're* not going to defend this place, who is? Besides, what are you going to do? Move to Florida?"

"Probably."

"No," Nina gasped.

"When I'm in a wheelchair," her mother added.

"What's the second thing I could do?"

"Talk to Kathy Silver. Find out what really happened. Confront Herb Silver if you have to."

"Great. Ma, I got a look at that man. He's like a male Leona Helmsley. And you know how effective I am in dealing with those kinds of guys." Nina had a rich-old-Jewish-man phobia. All those years in Housing Court, with the landlords and the landlords' lawyers, had only made it worse. She was incapable of withstanding the attacks of any Jewish man over sixty who was worth seven figures. Just being in their proximity was enough to reduce her to an inarticulate jellyfish.

"I know," Ida said. "I'm not exactly crazy about them either." Which was probably why she had married Nina's fa-

ther, a very intelligent man with a tendency to remain judg-
ment-proof.

"But you're right, Ma. I've gone this far, I should probably go all the way. I feel like I owe it to Lisa."

"It's up to you." Mothers were always saying "it's up to
you" in a way that made it clear that they didn't realize that
everything had been up to you for the past two decades.

Nina sucked down the last cold noodles. "So it looks like
it wasn't Beverly, after all," she said. "How do you feel about
that?"

"Relieved."

"Relieved? Are you kidding? You were the one who was
pointing a finger at her the entire time. All that stuff about
the widow with the smoking gun."

"I know, I was wrong. But it's easy to bet on someone
like Beverly. Hating her comes so naturally, almost as if she
were created to incur wrath. Like Joan Collins on *Dynasty*. She
made such a good villainess. Born to be loathed."

"So how come you're relieved to find out that she had
nothing to do with her husband's death?" Nina asked.

"Because deep down I wonder."

"Wonder what?"

"Wonder how different she is from me."

Nina gave her mother a hard look. "Pretty different, I'd
say. For one thing, your nails are about half the length of
hers. Not to mention your legs."

"Not to mention my legs is always a good idea."

"Seriously, do you really relate to Beverly Hirsch?"

"In a way," Ida said.

"In what way?"

"Well, I see her as just another Jewish girl, put on this
earth without benefit of wealth or privilege, working with
what God gave her."

"God? Who's that?" Nina asked.

"Okay. Fate. Working with what fate gave her. Like me."

"Like you?"

"In her case it was a fabulous body and big black hair and an ability to make men want to get into bed with her. In my case, it was being able to pass Latin at Hunter College and to teach reading to thirty-five kids at a time, while raising two of my own."

"I'm not sure I see a comparison."

"Why not?" Ida said. "If I could have ensured my well-being by simply seeing to it that I looked good, I might have skipped the master's degree and gone straight to Elizabeth Arden."

"So you think that you and Beverly are sisters under the skin?"

"Sisters under the nail polish. You don't feel that way?"

"No," said Nina. "I find her too threatening. Whenever I'm in a room with her, I can't help but reassess all my physical attributes, and I always come up short. Literally."

"You shouldn't feel that way. You have your own package and it's serving you pretty well, I think."

"You do?"

"I do," Ida said.

"Hmm. Maybe."

"Absolutely."

Nina thought about it. Perhaps her mother was right. Here she was, ambivalent about her career, no husband or children, living in an old-law tenement, practically having an anxiety attack every time she had to decide between kreplach and matzah balls in her soup. But if she searched her soul, she'd have to admit that she wouldn't change places with anyone. Not Beverly Hirsch, not her sister Laura, not any of the parade of women she trotted out to torture herself with.

Except maybe Meryl Streep.

32 . . . .

Nina was getting some funny looks, even though she had spent all morning constructing an outfit that she hoped looked inconspicuous. But she had clearly done something wrong, though she didn't know quite what. You would think that black footless tights, a long-sleeved black leotard, and Avia aerobic shoes would fit right in. But she was missing something—maybe shoulder pads, maybe more color. She felt like a lone, pale beatnik, sitting in the corner banging on her bongos, while the rest of the campus pranced around in circle pins and madras.

The members of this Great Neck gym weren't wearing madras, but they were wearing colors. There was a lot of Lycra in citrusy shades like lime-green, lemon-yellow, mandarin-orange—the kind of colors in which almost no one looked good. But someone had successfully manipulated the media and made them hot. At least for a season. The layered look had also hit; separates seemed to be big news in the activewear world. Everyone wore little halters and shorts and vestlike things that made Nina's black leotard look as old-fashioned as a corduroy jumper.

Beverly had gotten Nina a guest pass to Kathy Silver's gym. She had decided she'd rather deal with her than take on the father-in-law right off the bat. Nina supposed that she could have just marched right up to the Silvers' house and asked Kathy for a chat in the kitchen. But a confrontation in a public place seemed less threatening. Even if she had to do it in a leotard and tights.

Beverly said that if you hung around the gym long enough, Kathy was bound to show up there. She was a regular on a daily basis. So here was Nina after three hours, sitting in the lounge area right outside the women's locker room, monitoring a parade of big hair, trying to recognize a woman she had only caught a glimpse of once. To make things more difficult, the locker room had a front and back door. So the women entered one way in their street clothes, and exited out the back suited up to sweat. By the time Nina caught sight of them, they all gave off the same spandex glow. It was hard to tell them apart. Luckily, there was very little naturally blond hair around, so Nina had something to watch for.

She was momentarily thrown off by a fine-boned, fair-skinned woman in a yellow-and-pink striped unitard (unitards seemed to be acceptable alternatives to separates). But upon closer inspection, the hair turned out to be high-lighted. Dazzling and shiny, but chemically dependent none-theless. Not the real thing. Finally, Kathy did show up, look-ing not at all as Nina remembered. Fortunately, she was wearing her *chai*, which was large enough to catch Nina's eye.

Kathy Silver was clearly a subscriber to the layered look. She wore white bicycle shorts, topped by a black pullover that stopped a good four inches short of her bottoms. Over it was a zebra-patterned sleeveless garment that looked like a wrestling doublet. It plunged low enough to reveal an acute triangle of flesh at her midriff.

All in all, Kathy made a bold fashion statement. Nina thought back to the day when she realized that she would have to spend the rest of her life in black tights and retired her pink ones. A year later, she came to her senses and gave up ballet entirely. She remembered the decision clearly, as if it were yesterday. She had been six years old.

"Kathy?" Nina called out to her, trying to maintain eye contact, but was distracted by the *chai* and the exposed triangle of midriff skin.

"Do I know you?" Kathy managed to look puzzled without looking vulnerable.

"We've met. But just once."

"Have we?" Kathy smiled graciously. "I'm sorry, but I just can't recall."

"Nina Fischman," she said extending her hand.

Kathy digested the information slowly, as if translating a foreign language. "Oh, yes," she said as recognition dawned. "Are you a member here?" She took a sharp look at Nina's plain-Jane exercise outfit. When did leotards go out of style, anyway? Nina wondered.

"No, of course not. I live in the city. Actually, I came here looking for you."

"Then you're looking for the wrong person."

"Excuse me?"

"I had nothing to do with it."

"With what?" Nina tried to appear genuinely confused.

"Don't pretend you don't know exactly what I'm talking about." Boy, she was certainly cutting to the chase.

"I see."

"Good." Kathy addressed her straight ahead, without hesitation or apology. She bristled with fierce determination —which was something that Nina had always wanted to bristle with. She felt a surge of admiration for the woman. She had to remind herself that it might be the tiniest bit misguided to admire a single-minded and passionate attempt to cover up a murder conspiracy.

"I'm just trying to understand what happened here," Nina said. "Not because I have an exaggerated sense of justice. And not out of nosiness. But because Mark's daughter is suffering greatly, and I thought that if—"

"I don't give a shit," said Kathy. And it was clear that she didn't. She was protecting herself and her children, her home, her marriage. And that was all that mattered. Lisa Hirsch was outside of her sphere. And any lofty notions of community or sisterhood or justice were just so much static, interference to be blocked out.

Maybe it wasn't admiration Nina felt, so much as awe. It must make you feel powerful, Nina thought, to have such clearly defined boundaries. To know you had only a few square yards to protect, instead of an ill-defined terrain that sometimes seemed to stretch off into another cosmos.

Nina had the most ill-defined terrain of anyone she knew. She had some vague sense that it was important to get to the bottom of Mark Hirsch's murder, but she didn't know why. The item had somehow found its way onto her agenda, but then, her agenda had always been a joke. It was a long list of crossed-out and faded items, many with question marks next to them. How much simpler to have a short list written in bold strokes: stay rich, stay thin, and stay married. And make sure your kids get everything.

Nina plunged in again, but she knew she was on a losing ticket. "I can't, in all good conscience, simply—"

"Look, take your conscience and get out of my life. I told you, I have nothing to say to you."

How did Nina and Kathy get to be so different? Kathy's approach was the simpler to understand. She was clearly haunted by the image of her mother waitressing in a truck stop, with swollen feet and a weary heart. But Nina had her own haunting childhood images. Everyone did. Yet somehow hers had never galvanized her into transforming herself into a lean, mean machine, warily guarding her turf and greedily looking to annex some more.

Somewhere along the way, Nina had gotten the impression that she belonged to the world and the world belonged to her. And everything that happened to anybody anywhere was a concern. It made it hard to prioritize.

She didn't know how she had gotten this way. It was easy to blame being childless, but that wasn't the answer. Her mother had raised two children without escaping the syndrome. And she knew plenty of people without kids who confined their concerns to whether or not their cleaning lady was doing a good job.

It wasn't as if Nina were some saint running off to help the lepers or anything. She had a do-good job, but most of the time she wished she worked for a magazine, writing articles on fingernail polish or wall sconces. But the words that Kathy had just spoken—I don't give a shit—were ones that never left Nina's lips. When she searched her soul, she couldn't come up with one single thing that she completely and honestly didn't give a shit about.

"Do you think it might be helpful for me to talk to your father-in-law?" Nina asked.

"Why don't you do that? He's in North Shore Hospital. It's right near here, over on Community Drive. Visiting hours go until eight o'clock. I'm sure he'd appreciate the company." Kathy straightened herself up and pulled the crotch of her zebra-patterned whatever-it-was out of her crack and down over her buttocks. "One thing, though. Before you go."

"What's that?"

"I'd change if I were you," Kathy said. And laughed in a mean way that brought Nina right back to her eighth-grade gym class.

33 ....

Herb Silver was sitting up in bed, playing with the remote control clicker. He was doing a quick scan, spending no more than ten seconds on each television channel. Nina recognized the syndrome as a common male affliction. But she hadn't realized that it struck men of all ages, even a generation that had grown up listening to Fred Allen on the radio. It had been misguided to think that it plagued only the television generation. A remote-control attention deficit was clearly something you could develop later in life.

His silvery hair was wilder than the last time she'd seen him. It made him look something like Leonard Bernstein, sort of leonine. Also narcissistic. Herb Silver was now letting the remote control linger on *Entertainment Tonight,* so Nina took the opportunity to step into the room and announce herself.

"Hello, Mr. Silver. I'm—"

"Oh, finally." He cut her off. "I've been waiting all evening for you."

"I doubt it," she said.

"Aren't you the girl they sent to bring me some books? I'm sick of this goddamn idiot box."

"No, I'm not here about books."

"Well, you look like someone who would be here about books." Nina tried to picture herself as a glamorous fiction editor, sort of a female Michael Korda. But she knew what Silver meant. She was a woman who wore flat shoes and didn't lighten her hair. And her Navajo earrings weren't sufficient to disabuse him of his perception of her as a mousy librarian. "What are you here about? Not bringing more fruit, I hope," he said, glancing at her tote bag, which held her mousy librarian's leotard. "Because I don't need any more. I've got enough fruit to give me the runs into the next century." He waved a hand around the room, which contained not only three fruit baskets but a dried rose topiary bush, a bunch of Mylar balloons floating on the ceiling, a six-foot-long computer printout tacked along one wall that said "Get Well Soon, Grandpa" and a couple of floral arrangements in various stages of wilt. "Not that I'll make it into the next century," he went on. "They don't seem so sure that I'll make it into the next month."

"I'm sorry to hear that."

"Why are you sorry to hear that? Who are you, anyway? You look familiar. Who sent you? The office? My wife? Oh, I recognize you now. Samantha's teacher, right? I met you at her school play, didn't I?"

Oh, great. If she wasn't a mousy librarian, maybe she was a mousy schoolteacher. She decided to cut this game short. "I'm not Samantha's teacher, but we did meet once. At your son's house. My name is Nina Fischman and I've come to discuss the death of Mark Hirsch with you." She paused for effect, but Silver remained silent. "He was your son's business—"

"I know who he was," he interrupted. "I know goddamn well who he was. He was a crook and a con artist, that's who he was."

The television blared on. Mary Hart started to announce the day's birthdays, which meant that it was getting close to eight o'clock. She'd get thrown out of here soon. "Can we turn this off?"

"*I* can turn it off," he said, giving the clicker a violent twist. "Don't give me this *we* crap. I get *we*d to death all day around here. Do *we* want some orange juice? Do *we* want to take our medicine? I can't stand it anymore." He clicked off the television. "Now, who are you again?" She was sure he was asking just to bug her.

Who was she again? Indeed. Sometimes it was hard to remember. "I'm a friend of the Hirsch family. They're all very upset about Mark's death."

"Oh, yeah? Including that wife of his? She looks like she'll get over it pretty fast."

"Well, his daughter won't. Look, Mr. Silver, I think I know quite a bit about what went on. I just need to tie up a few loose ends. You know you don't have to cooperate with me. I'm not a law enforcement official. I can't subpoena you. I can't take you in for questioning."

"You certainly can't. For one thing, I'm not portable," he said, lifting an arm that was connected to an intravenous tube.

"I see that. Well, as I said, I can't force you to cooperate. But from what I hear, it seems as though you don't have that much to lose."

"Ha. So they tell me. You know, four months ago, I thought I had everything to lose. I'd turned seventy last year, but I could still beat my son at tennis. The business seemed recession-proof. We were going to start exporting upholstery fabric to Eastern Europe. My grandchildren actually liked me, or at least they seemed to. And I had just put down a deposit on a place in Boca. Then they send me in for some routine surgery, a little prostate problem. Nothing major, every man my age seems to have it."

"And what happened?"

"They tell me I'm riddled with tumors. Can you believe it? Me? Herb Silver?"

"I can't really say. After all, I don't know you very well."

"Take it from me, I haven't been sick a day in my life. I stopped going to the dentist thirty years ago and I haven't had a toothache since."

"I guess cancer can happen to anyone. Even the strongest and the healthiest."

"Well, it happened to me. In a big way. And there doesn't seem to be anything they can do about it. Just keep me here and feebly poke and prod me every now and then."

"You look pretty good." He certainly wasn't having any trouble projecting.

"I have my good days and my bad days. You caught me on a good one, Mrs. Epstein."

"Uh, it's Fischman. Ms."

"Oh, right. I think Epstein is the name of Samantha's drama teacher. Anyway, Mrs. Fischman, let me explain something to you about what went on with that Hirsch boy. When you find yourself in a position such as I am, nothing else seems worth making a big *tsimmis* out of. Your daughter-in-law calls you, she's all upset about something or other. And you know that you can take care of the whole thing with just a phone call. So you do it. That was all that Mark Hirsch was— a business problem that got taken care of with a phone call."

"He was more than that, Mr. Silver. He was a human being, somebody's father."

"Really, Mrs. Fischman, I don't give a shit. I didn't then and I don't now." An interesting bunch, these Silvers. The family that didn't give a shit. "One thing I do want to make clear. Kathy had nothing really to do with it. She came to me with the problem. I was the one who came up with the solution."

Was he covering for her? Steve had said that Kathy and Herb were powerful allies. For all Nina knew, Kathy Silver could have pushed Mark over the hill with her own two hands and convinced her father-in-law to take the rap.

Was it worth figuring out exactly what happened? Would it really help Lisa? Could anything really help Lisa? Maybe a new mother. And a change of scenery. Get her into a zip code where people didn't weigh themselves twice a day.

"I think visiting hours are over," Nina said. She pulled a business card out of her purse. "If there's anything you'd like to discuss further, please call me."

Silver took the card and looked at it. "You're a lawyer?" She nodded. "And all this time, I thought you taught school. Didn't you tell me you were a schoolteacher?"

"Oh, please, Mr. Silver. I didn't tell you any such thing. But it doesn't really matter, does it? Because you probably haven't heard one word I've said. Men like you never listen to women like me. We're not rich, we're not glamorous, it's like we don't exist. Well, let me tell you something. Women like me are going to law school in greater numbers than ever before. And a lot of us are becoming prosecutors. And that means we get to see that megalomaniacal scofflaws like yourself get to rot in jail. And those of us that choose to practice civil as opposed to criminal law get to sue the pants off you." A thought suddenly occurred to Nina. "There's a wrongful death action here, you know. One that could eat up your entire estate. Including your granddaughter's goddamn horse." She turned to leave.

"Hoo ha," he said as she stormed out. Maybe *hoo ha* was how he felt, but she felt a lot better.

34 . . . .

It was one of those fluky days in March that make you think that winter is actually receding. It's always a cruel hoax, of course, with a freezing rain right around the corner. But today was warm enough to tempt even the most cautious out of their caves, so Nina and Lisa ventured forth into the sunshine. A walk in the park was in order, Nina thought, as they left the Loews Eighty-fourth Street Sixplex.

Ida had thought it nice that Nina had offered Lisa lunch and a movie. But it wasn't charity work, she had assured her mother. You couldn't force a yenta to do something that she didn't find inherently interesting. Lisa did interest her, and the fact that Nina actually liked and had generous impulses toward her came second.

"Can we go to Strawberry Fields?" Lisa asked.

"Sure." It was the part of Central Park across from the Dakota, the apartment building where John Lennon had lived and died. Yoko Ono had arranged for a couple of acres to be planted with all sorts of exotic horticultural specimens.

There was a big marble plaque that had IMAGINE written in brass letters.

"And then can we go and look at the Dakota?" Lisa asked.

"Okay." It was amazing that he still had a hold on these kids' imaginations. Kids that were too young to remember him alive. There was always a scruffy knot of blue-jeaned adolescents outside the Dakota on any given weekend.

They headed south on Broadway. Lisa was wearing her usual mix of Miracle Mile and Canal Jeans. This time her outfit included a pair of overalls with one strap unhooked. It was a fad that had started with the city's ghetto youth and had apparently spread to Great Neck South High School. Lisa also carried a fake Chanel quilted shoulder bag, with chains for straps. Nina had always hated Chanel instinctively. When she found out that Coco Chanel had based her designs on the uniforms of her lover, a high-ranking Nazi officer, Nina felt vindicated, that she had been right all along.

"Did you know that Samantha's grandfather is dying?"

"You mean Herb Silver? Steve's father?"

"Uh-huh."

"I heard. And how are Steve and Kathy doing?" Nina asked.

"Who knows? My mother said she saw her at the gym the other day and Kathy told her she was going to Morocco for a week without Steve."

"Why would she want to go to Morocco?"

"Shopping."

"In Morocco?"

"Oh yeah. Didn't you know that? All my mother's friends go to Marrakech for the pocketbooks and leather clothing. They make great designer knockoffs and they're a fraction of the price compared to France or Italy."

"I didn't know." Morocco had always been a traveler's

paradise. Gay men used to go there for the young boys. Hippies used to go there for the hashish. Nina had once gone there and come back with hennaed hair. Now Long Island women went there for the leather goods. It was a little hard to picture, but Nina supposed that if someone could find their way around the Lexington Avenue branch of Bloomingdale's, they could find their way around the Casbah.

"So what have you been up to?" Nina asked.

"Nothing."

"What did you think of the movie?"

"It was okay."

"Some of the scenes were great. But the end, when Mia Farrow leaves Bill Hurt and moves downtown . . . well, I thought it was a bit much. She becomes like the Greenwich Village equivalent of Mother Teresa. Meanwhile, she's living off of her husband's alimony."

"Yeah." Lisa was silent for a moment. "I think that my mother's going to marry Stuart Grossman. His divorce is almost final. And she's been spending a lot of time talking about rings lately."

"Is that going to be terrible for you?"

"Not really. I don't see that it's going to make much difference. He's over there all the time now anyway."

"Whatever happens, I hope things work out okay for you." Nina wanted to say something reassuring, something about some girls peaking in adolescence and then going into a slow decline. While for others, life just gets easier and easier. And the torment fades into a long-ago bad dream. But Nina didn't quite feel like a poster girl for late bloomers. "It does get better," she added, sending out a feeler.

"That's easy for you to say. You have everything you want."

"I do?"

"Don't you?"

"To some extent. Compared to somebody living in Iraq, I guess I do." Or compared to a chubby adolescent living in Manhasset Hills with Beverly Hirsch.

They turned east on Seventy-second Street and both paused involuntarily in front of the Eclair Bakery. "Want to get something to eat?" Lisa asked.

"Not if you're going to throw it up." It was out before Nina had a chance to think about it. "We can come back later," she said, more gently. "Let's go to the park before it gets dark."

"I stopped doing that," Lisa said. "I haven't done it in weeks."

"Well, that's good."

"It's good, except that I'm blowing up like a balloon."

"You look exactly the same to me. Besides, I don't like women who keep telling me how fat they are. If you're going to be one of them, I'm not going to hang around with you."

"But it's true."

"Look, you are not thin. And unless you devote your life to it, you probably never will be. And not everyone can devote their life to it. Some of us have better things to do." Nina gave an impudent sniff, very Mary Poppins. "But that doesn't mean that you are doomed to a life of misery. For one thing, you have such a pretty—" My God, she had almost said it. What was happening to her? "For one thing," she started again, "you were born at the right time. Into an age when women are judged on things other than how thin they are. You were, however, born in the wrong place. From this you can escape."

"What do you mean?"

"I mean Long Island. A place where women seem to be judged mostly on weight and length of nails."

"Oh, come on," Lisa said. "It's not so bad. There are

actually some pretty decent people out there. Besides, what's so great about New York City?"

"I'll show you." They crossed the street and entered Strawberry Fields. Then Nina turned Lisa around, facing toward the Hudson River, and pointed to the architecture of Central Park West. The dark turrets of the Dakota dominated the foreground. Down at the end of Seventy-second Street, the sky was pink over the river. "Pretty neat, huh?"

"Yeah, pretty neat." A furry gray rodent scurried across their path and disappeared into Strawberry Fields. "Nina, that wasn't a squirrel, was it?"

"No." Another one ran by. "We've got a pretty bad infestation problem in Central Park," Nina admitted. "We're just loaded with rats."

"It makes it pretty hard to appreciate the rest of it."

"Lisa, you can't focus on the rats. If you do, you'll spend your life with your head in the toilet bowl."

"So what do you do? Pretend that you don't see them?"

"Do I strike you as the kind of woman who pretends that I don't see things?"

"I don't know. I guess not."

Nina reached over and pushed Lisa's hair out of her eyes. This time she said it. "You have such a pretty face." And as soon as it came out, Nina realized that all those ladies really had meant it. They had thought she had a pretty face. And at that precise moment Nina knew that she had slipped over some invisible line into middle age.

35 . . . . . .

"Apparently," said Tom, putting his feet up on Nina's coffee table, "Herb Silver took the rap for the whole thing. Said it was all his idea, that his daughter-in-law had nothing to do with it."

"And who actually pushed the car off the road?" Nina asked.

"A couple of punks who had just gotten out of Dannemora. Unfortunately our town gets some ex-cons on their way south, looking for work of any kind. Old Herb had some good connections. He knew plenty of people upstate. He spends every August at Saratoga. At the track."

"Lisa said that the family was into horses. That Steve's kid has one of her own."

"How is Lisa? Have you been keeping in touch?"

"I guess she's okay, pretty much. I wish I could say that finding out the truth about her father's death has helped with some of her unresolved conflicts and that she's turned into one happy sunbeam of an adolescent. But I don't think it goes that way."

"No, not usually."

"I myself have always considered resolved conflict to be an oxymoron," she said. Trying to show off her neuroses to Tom was unfair. She had an advantage, her people had an extra couple of thousand years of practice. Nina changed the subject. "Was what Herb Silver said about being terminally ill really true?"

"It looks that way. Riddled with cancer, tumors the size of grapefruits, all that."

"Do you think that people really mean what they say about tumors being the size of grapefruits?" Nina asked. "They're never as big as a lemon or an orange or a persimmon. It's always a grapefruit. What I want to know is how come they're all the same size. It sounds pretty suspicious to me."

"They're not even bothering to give him chemotherapy, according to what I've heard."

"Has he been formally charged?"

"Yeah. He's negotiating some kind of plea, but he'll never do any time. His next move is probably into a hospice."

"And the ex-cons?"

"You know how the criminal justice system works. The prosecutor is using Herb Silver's testimony to put the squeeze on the cons. And using those two to put the squeeze on some other guys who pulled some kind of bank job in Albany. And on and on it goes."

"And it all happened the way we thought?"

"Exactly. They got Hirsch dead drunk, put him in the car, started the engine, and pushed him over the hill. Just like that. The cops did mess up on one thing, though."

"I thought they were hiding something. What was it?"

"Skid marks. They should have been able to tell from the

absence of skid marks that the car was pushed. But they hadn't bothered to check. And of course it was too late by the time we got to the scene."

"Well, send my regards to Mel," Nina said, "when you go back."

"Aw, do I have to go back?"

"Not as far as I'm concerned." She lifted her face up to his and looked into his eyes. They were still hooded and a little bloodshot, even though he had left his marijuana at home. She didn't care. He looked good to her.

So far the weekend had been all she had hoped for. Not quite up there with New Hampshire, but close. For one thing, their affair had been reconsummated on her couch. She always had the best sex on her couch, even though it was a lumpy old thing. She must have some sort of vestigial territorial erotic impulse that kicked in only when she was on her own turf. And her couch was better than her bed. It gave it a bit of an illicit thrill, she supposed, the way some people could only get it on in elevators.

Tom and Nina didn't seem to need an elevator. They were doing just fine, having spent the past two days mostly on the couch, partially dressed, pulling on socks or a shirt when an extremity got cold. Having long, unresolved conversations about whether it was worth the trouble of getting dressed to go out and get something to eat. And here it was Sunday afternoon, and Tom was still talking. A good sign. Perhaps they had gotten over some sort of hump.

But she knew that Tom would soon be hitting the road and she would have to start obsessing about when she'd see him again. To distract herself, she leaned forward and kissed him. He put his arms around Nina and pulled her closer. They sank back into the pillows. "Great couch," he said. "I could stay on it forever."

"That would be nice," she said, pulling up her T-shirt to maximize contact.

A minute later the phone rang. She let it go, waiting for the machine to kick in. It wasn't until the sixth ring that she remembered that she had forgotten to release the pause button yesterday. She reached over carefully, managing not to dislodge Tom's mouth from her breast, and picked it up. "Hello?" she said, knowing she sounded a little breathy.

"What's the matter?" Ida said. "Is everything all right? You sound preoccupied."

"Not preoccupied. Occupied."

It was a nice change, Nina thought as she hung up.